SOMEWHERE ON MACKINAC

AN M/M ROMANCE

JEFF ADAMS

Somewhere on MACKINAC

Jeff Adams

SOMEWHERE ON MACKINAC

How far would you go for the man of your dreams?

Now that he's single, Chicago businessman Jordan Monroe can finally take his long-desired trip to Mackinac Island for the *Somewhere In Time* fan celebration weekend. On the first day, Jordan finds himself attracted to Miles Colter, a handsome, local stable owner who is giving horseback tours of the film's locations.

Jordan is surprised and charmed that Miles pursues him. When Jordan learns the stable is in trouble, he wants to help despite Miles's resistance. As their relationship grows personally and professionally, Jordan dreads the issues that face them—an ex who won't let him go, the complications of a long-distance relationship, and a secret he knows he shouldn't be keeping.

Can Jordan and Miles find a way to forge a love as timeless as the romance in their favorite film?

Somewhere on Mackinac
Copyright © 2017 by Jeff Adams
All rights reserved.

Editor: Kiki Clark, LesCourt Author Services
Cover Design: Alexandria Corza, seeingstatic.com

2nd edition, 2020 from Big Gay Media
1st edition, 2017 from Dreamspinner Press

Somewhere on Mackinac is a work of fiction. Names, characters, places, brands, and incidents are solely the product of the author's imagination and/or are used fictitiously, though reference may be made to actual historical events or existing locations. Any resemblance to actual persons, living or dead, is entirely coincidental.

No part of this book may be reproduced in any form or by any electronic or mechanical means, including information storage and retrieval systems, without written permission from the author, except for the use of brief quotations in a book review.

ONE

Leave it to Drake to make the start of vacation annoying.

"Come on, Jordan, how could you just go solo?" Drake's voice boomed through the car's speakers. "How's it going to look to our colleagues that you've gone off to a romantic weekend on your own?"

Unbelievable. He hadn't wanted me to go on this trip last year when we were a couple, and he was still trying to spoil it.

I clicked the controls on the steering wheel to lower the volume. His agitated voice was a stark contrast to the calm, peaceful, rural landscape of Michigan. It was a perfect fall day and ideal for driving the Mackinaw Trail, also known by its far less sexy name of US 131. Until the phone call, I'd been cruising along and enjoying the farmland, mostly bare trees, and lack of traffic.

Five hours north of Chicago and everything was perfect —at least until Drake had called and interrupted my music shuffle of love songs. I should've sent the call to voice mail.

"Why do you care?" I forced myself to be calm since I wasn't interested in playing the game where he expected everyone to match his level of distress. It was one of the reasons I'd broken it off with him. His ongoing need for drama wore me out. I was still connected to him because of business ties, though. Drake's firm and mine shared several clients and often made referrals to each other.

"Sometimes I don't understand you," he said, exasperated.

That wasn't an answer. He used one of his go-to phrases for getting people to feel bad about their choices.

"The feeling's mutual," I muttered, not caring if he heard.

"When will you be back?"

"Tuesday, maybe Wednesday."

Silence.

"The Cooper dinner is Monday night."

"Yeah, and Alberto has that covered."

"Our firms bought the table together. We can't have an empty chair. And you're one of the partners."

"Alberto has someone for my chair too." Annoyance crept into my voice. "This trip has been on my calendar since right after you bailed on it last year."

"I'll come up with an excuse." He sounded even more annoyed. In a weird way, he seemed to enjoy being upset.

"That's not your place. Alberto will speak for me and the firm."

"There's no way we can tell people you've gone off to an island to celebrate some sappy movie." He ignored what I said.

"Tell them whatever you want." My thumb played over the disconnect button. I needed to get back to enjoying the drive and my playlist. "I gotta go."

"Jord—"

I hung up.

I'd heard about the *Somewhere in Time* weekend at the Grand Hotel on Mackinac Island three years ago. It was mentioned in the extras on the collector's edition DVD. It sounded incredible—staying at the Grand where the movie had been filmed, tours of the locations, panels with some of the stars and filmmakers, a gala costume ball, horse-and-buggy rides, and more. It was the perfect opportunity to geek out on one of my favorite films.

The Grand Hotel looked like a gorgeous place to spend a few days. To add to the charm, it was on an island in the middle of the Michigan straits. You could only get to Mackinac by ferry or small plane. No cars were allowed, despite what the movie showed, and the setting was idyllic. To this day, the island looked like something out of the past.

I was staying past the film festivities for the Grand's end-of-season closing ceremony. I'd read about the ceremony and decided it'd be cool to be part of that too.

I'd fallen hard for the 1980 film when I'd seen it in '96. I'd been home sick from school and channel surfing when I'd come across it. Christopher Reeve was a major crush for me, and he'd drawn me into the movie. I'd loved him in the first two *Superman* movies. *Deathtrap* was incredible and where my crush had formed.

Somewhere in Time had seemed kinda hokey at first—the idea of time traveling with your mind seemed silly. But the sheer romance of going back to find your true love had swept me away. By the end of the movie, I'd been sobbing because he'd died of a broken heart.

I'd liked the film the first time I'd watched it, but it was the second viewing that had started my obsession. At the start of the film, Elise walked up to Richard in present day 1980, said "Come back to me," and left him a pocket watch. He had no clue about her because he hadn't time traveled yet. It was one of the most powerful things I'd seen in a movie. For her, Richard's love lasted forever.

It was hard to explain to people why I like this movie. Even more difficult was discussing the plot with anyone who hadn't seen it. People can have a hard time with time travel and romance together. It worked for this movie, though.

After Richard got the watch, he was haunted by the woman who gave it to him. Eventually, he discovered she was an actress from 1912. As he learned more, he was possessed to get to her. Reading about a theoretical way to travel back in time using the power of the mind and hypnosis was *the* answer.

I've been a romantic ever since that movie, and those stories became my go-to for movies or books. *Somewhere in Time* spoke to me about finding your one true love and how that was timeless. I wanted to feel all the emotions that flooded me when I watched the movie—the hope as Richard met Elise the first time, the spark they shared dancing, their growing attraction, and immense happiness with each other. I didn't want the crushing heartbreak they had, but it showed me how intense their bond was. That was the heart of the story.

Even at sixteen, I knew I wanted a love like that. I'd had four serious boyfriends since then, and none of them had been *that* love. I'd met Drake at a reception for a mutual business contact. It seemed we'd had a lot in common, and the first five or six months were great. There was lots of romance and wooing on both sides. I was happy.

But after that, it felt more like we were settling into a business partnership than a romance. I worked at fixing our relationship as much as I could, but sometimes the status quo won out. Over time, it became clear that Drake was interested in getting ahead and appearances more than anything else. While I was usually willing to go along with what he wanted to do to help keep the peace, he was less amenable.

I shook my head vigorously. Fixating on where Drake and I went wrong wasn't going to accomplish anything. I was on my way to a fabulous weekend, which I hoped would help me rekindle my desire for romance. Drake and I broke up after weeks of fighting, and since then, I'd been skittish about starting anything. I didn't expect to find love this weekend, but I hoped it would at least get me ready to start dating again.

In some ways, the movie is so simple, if you look past the time travel. Two people drawn together for reasons they don't even understand. They pushed back against those keeping them apart and formed a bond for all time. I wanted that when I was sixteen. Now that I was closer to forty, I wanted it even more—the romance, a soul mate, maybe a family.

I clicked the voice dial on the wheel.

"Call Alberto."

"Calling Alberto Belasco," the voice responded.

"Please tell me you're not still in the city," Alberto said, in lieu of a greeting.

"Nope. Left early this morning."

"Excellent."

Alberto was my best friend and business partner. We'd met while we were in business school, working on our MBAs. A group project bonded us, and while we'd worked separately for a few years after graduation, we'd finally formed our own business-consulting firm four years ago. Belasco & Monroe had a good reputation, and we had a waiting list of clients who wanted to work with us.

"So what brings this call on your vacation?"

"Drake was being a dick, and I wanted to vent before I finished the drive."

I spelled out the conversation I'd had just minutes before.

"You know I've got the Cooper dinner covered, right?"

"I have complete faith. You know how he gets caught up on things that don't matter."

"I think he sees it as a chance to maybe woo you back. You guys met at a business gig after all."

"Really? He's been seeing other guys. Why would he be trying to get me back after six months?"

"Having seen the seating chart for our table, I know he's not bringing anyone. Despite your troubles, I'd say he's fixated."

"Oh, good." Sarcasm spilled out as I rolled my eyes.

"Let it go, man. You're on vacation. It's gonna be great, and when you get back, you'll be relaxed and ready to get out there again."

"Hopefully it'll be that easy."

Alberto gave a "huh-uh" with some attitude that made me smile.

"Listen, would you mind if I turned the phone off when I get to the island? I can't have it out during events since the organizers are trying to keep an authentic feeling to the weekend and neither 1980 nor 1912 had iPhones. Plus, I don't want to leave myself open for other annoying phone calls."

"Not at all," Alberto said. "I can't imagine I'll need to track you down over the next few days. If I do, I can go old-school, call the hotel, and leave you a very quaint message."

We laughed. Alberto's sense of humor was one of the

reasons he was such a great friend and business partner. Few things stressed him out.

"Thanks," I said.

"But, if you decide to time travel, let me know so I don't wonder where you are next week."

"Deal. You'll be the first to know."

"And I'll remind you not to travel with any rogue pennies."

"I would hope so."

His laughter put me in exactly the mindset I needed—carefree.

"Okay," he said. "I'm hanging up, and you're turning the phone off."

"Later, man."

I disconnected the call and was happy to put aside that aspect of the modern world.

TWO

To get to the island, I'd decided to take the ferry from St. Ignace because I wanted to go over the bridge, a five mile span connecting the upper and lower peninsulas. It was a beautiful fall day with just a few wispy clouds scattered across the sky. The shining sun turned the waters of Lake Michigan and Lake Huron a gorgeous blue that sparkled.

Going over the bridge was exhilarating, and more than a little scary. I'd never been on such a long bridge. Pain shot through my hands because of how tightly I gripped the steering wheel as I drove. I'd read that if it was gusty, the bridge could sway. I appreciated that the wind was light because I didn't need swaying on my first, already nerve-racking, crossing.

As I drove off the bridge, I laughed at myself and my apprehension eased. It'd been an easy drive, and yet I tensed up like it was the scariest thing ever. Sometimes I wondered why my brain reacted like it did. I'd wanted to drive over the bridge, and I'd enjoyed it, but, man, I got riled up doing it.

The sixteen minutes on the ferry was a stark contrast to

the bridge. Even though it was chilly, I stood on deck to watch the island approach. It was the perfect transition from mainland to island. As we cut across the lake, the island's trees were visible. Horses and bikes traveling the road that ran along the island's edge came into view as we got closer.

I relaxed against the railing on the side of the boat with several other travelers. Many were below in the enclosed cabin, but I had more than a dozen people on deck with me. I knew that arriving a day early was the right choice so I could explore on my own before the activities started.

Eventually, the small city became visible with houses and other buildings appearing ahead. I drew in a deep breath of clean, cool air and shuddered—not from the cold but because of the sheer satisfaction. I loved fall air, but this was probably as pure as it got.

Once the ferry swung around the southern end of the island, the true expanse was visible with piers and buildings crowding the shore. The mix of architecture styles was from a different time. I recognized many of the buildings were Shingle Style, which was supposed to be most prevalent on the island. I spotted several Greek Revivals and Colonials as well. I'd enjoyed the art and architecture appreciation classes I'd taken in college, and seeing these marvelous structures was inspiring.

As we disembarked, I only had my messenger bag with me. My luggage was tagged to go on to the hotel. I hung back and watched people leave instead of bustling off in the crowd. Once I got on to the pier, though, I'd never seen so many bicycles in one place. You could rent them as soon as you stepped off the boat, while others were locked up, waiting for their owners to return. This was the kind of parking lot you ended up with when there were no cars. I loved it. It spoke about the lifestyle the islanders had.

A few of the people I disembarked with went for bicycles. Some people simply left on foot for their destination. Others headed for the horse-drawn buggies standing by. I spotted one from the Grand Hotel and went there. Again, I shook with anticipation. First time in a horse-drawn carriage and I was giddy. Two horses stood at the ready as a man dressed in a black tux and top hat helped a family into the rear of the carriage. It didn't seem possible, but the carriage looked like it could be from a hundred years ago.

There were only four other people in the carriage, and we took off for the hotel. I didn't know where to look because I wanted to see everything—from the trees, to the lake, to bicycles and carriages sharing the road, and all the surroundings.

As we approached the hotel, I pressed my face against the window. It looked just like it had in the movie. Despite more than thirty-five years passing since the film was shot, the hotel had barely changed. I knew that'd be the case from seeing the hotel's website, but seeing it in person gave me goose bumps. It was silly. It was just a building, but it was a thrill to see a place I'd been familiar with for nearly half my life. An unexpected rush of emotions hit me, and I struggled for a moment to keep myself in check. I hadn't expected this to overwhelm me like that. I enjoyed it, though—it told me I needed to be here for this.

"Is this your first time here?" asked the woman sitting across from me.

I pulled back from the window, realizing I must have looked like a child. Embarrassing! I hadn't acknowledged my travel companions. I'd been too busy gawking at everything.

"Yes," I said. "I've been looking forward to this for months."

"Told you," the girl next to her said. "You can always spot the newbies."

"You're going to have a great time," the woman said. "I'm Melanie. These are my daughters, Angie and Cathy, and my husband, George."

I shook hands with George and nodded at the ladies. "Jordan," I said.

The daughters looked to be in their teens. One was busy with her phone while the other was resting against the seat back and watching the scenery pass by. They appeared to be a regular Midwestern family. I wouldn't have been surprised to come across them in a grocery store in suburban Chicago.

"My daughters and I love the movie." Melanie spoke with enthusiasm. "George plays golf most days but comes to some of the fancy evening gatherings."

"How many years have you done this?" I asked.

Melanie looked to George. "Six?"

"Sounds about right," he said. "Your wife joining you later?"

I shook my head slowly. "I'm here solo."

The daughter who'd been studying her phone looked up. "Gay?"

There was no malice in her voice. It was a simple question.

"Yeah," I said with a slight laugh. "That obvious?"

"Cathy," chastised Angie, who, I decided, must be the oldest, "that's rude."

"What?" Cathy laughed a little too. "How many men have we met here, traveling by themselves, who turned out not to be gay?"

"Please forgive my daughter." Melanie looked a touch horrified by the conversation.

"It's all right." I was barely able to contain my amusement. "I decided immersing myself in my favorite movie was a perfect way to spend a fall weekend. My boyfriend didn't want to come last year, and now that I'm single, I decided to treat myself."

Truth was, just being on the carriage was already making me wish I was sharing this with someone. There was no way I was going to admit that out loud to anyone, especially strangers.

"Good for you." Melanie nodded, allowing the awkwardness to pass.

"How's the golf here?" I turned to George.

"It's a good course. I usually get a couple of games in over the weekend. You're welcome to join me if you'd like. I usually try to build a foursome to go out."

"I might take you up that. I'm not great, but I enjoy it."

The carriage came to a stop at the front entrance, and I was in awe once again—that was probably going to be a constant state for the weekend. The hotel was over one hundred years old and one of the most incredible buildings I'd ever seen. I'd been to other places, like Provincetown, where there were older buildings, but this was breathtaking with its enormous porch, pristine white paint, handcrafted railings and moldings, and yellow awnings over each window. There were lots of pictures pleading to be snapped.

I allowed the family to leave the carriage first, then I stepped out and took a deep breath. I couldn't get over the air—so crisp and clean. I hadn't thought it'd get better than on the ferry, but here, there was a slight smell of flowers and horse. It was country air, and it flushed out the last part of the city from my blood. A switch had been flipped, and all my cares disappeared as I took in the grandeur of the hotel —and the spot on the porch where Richard had watched Elise run back to him after she'd been forced to leave.

I was here!

"It was nice to meet you," Melanie said.

"I'm sorry. It's all so amazing." I gestured at the hotel. "It was great meeting you all too."

"We'll see you around," George said. "Let me know if you want in for golf. I know I'll be going out tomorrow. Probably Saturday too since it looks like we're going to have great weather."

"I'll do that."

I climbed the steps and moved to the railing to be out of the way. The porch was incredible because it just went on and on. Looking out over the well-manicured grounds, scenes from the movie overlaid the landscape in my mind's eye.

I'm such a geek. I grinned as I walked inside. It might have been a good thing I was traveling solo. If I was going to get emotional and caught up in everything, it was better no one I knew saw me.

I looked around the lobby, taking in everything. I knew from my research that the lobby in the movie was downstairs, and I was going to have to check it out later. It didn't matter that this wasn't the movie lobby. I was freakin' here and about to check in.

I stepped up to the desk once the clerk finished up with Melanie and George.

"Good afternoon, sir. Checking in?"

The clerk was dressed to the nines and looked to be about my age. He carried himself with a dignity that fit the surroundings.

"Yes. Jordan Monroe."

"Welcome to the Grand Hotel." The clerk busied himself getting things together. "We have you in three-fourteen. There's also this packet of information from the weekend's organizers with the schedule. They'll be having general check-in tomorrow morning."

He handed me the packet and a key—an actual key. I couldn't remember the last time I'd stayed somewhere with a real key. I cradled it in my hand, rubbing my thumb over it. Everything was cards and fobs these days. A real key made it seem like the past, and I loved it.

"I see your luggage is arriving from the ferry, so we'll bring that to the room as soon as it's here. Is there anything else I can do for you?"

"No, thank you."

He smiled. "Very good. Enjoy your stay, and if you need anything, just let us know."

I nodded and headed off to my room. I wanted to get rid of my messenger bag and go explore. It was too nice to be indoors.

The room was nice. I went for a midlevel one because I liked more space than just a bed. This looked comfortable and would be more than sufficient for the weekend. I wasn't sure how much I'd use the couch and chair, but it was nice to have them along with the king bed. There were modern amenities, like a wide-screen TV, albeit small, and a minibar fridge. I was tempted to store them in the closet, as Richard did in the movie, to make the room look more 1912. That seemed a little over the top, though.

I dropped my bag on the couch and went out the French doors to the balcony where there were two lounge chairs and a table. I was on the back side of the hotel, but the lake was within view, as were some well-kept residential homes. We're talking magazine-cover quality with the landscaping and architecture. I wondered if it was as incredible to live in one of those as I thought it would be, or if it was all about the upkeep.

It'd be perfect to have a real romantic weekend here. A touch of sadness crept in, as happened every now and then since the breakup. I'd like to think I didn't *need* a man, but I did want to build a life with someone.

It was time to check this place out more thoroughly, so I headed for where I wanted to be—outside and the porch.

My breath caught as I looked across the lush green lawn and flowerbeds and on to the lake. I'd never been any place like this.

The breeze across the length of the porch was just right—not too gusty and not too chilly. Guests sat in the rocking chairs, enjoying the afternoon. At one end, two men played chess at an oversized board set into the porch. I headed toward the other end and the lake. When I finally got there, the view was of trees, water, and the bridge I'd just gone over a few hours before.

My breath caught as I saw the most stunning man. I didn't often see someone who was so handsome it made me stop. In my experience, those sorts of men existed only in the movies. Yet, he was just a few feet away on the other side of the flower boxes that marked the border of the porch. It was clear by the cut of his black pants and white shirt that he was sturdily built. He had close-cropped blond hair, just long enough that he could part it and lay it flat. Best of all, he sported a nicely trimmed beard. Few things caught my attention quite like a blond with a beard.

He walked with a horse, holding its reins, while he talked with a woman who wore riding clothes. They smiled and laughed as they went, enjoying the afternoon and each other's company. It didn't take long for them to pass out of view. I thought about jumping over the flowers to go after him. But then what?

Hi. I like your beard.

That was probably his girlfriend anyway, or wife. Lucky her.

Besides, even if it'd just been him walking on the path, hookups weren't my thing. Unless, of course, I could be lucky enough that he happened to be single and from Chicago and he was just friends with the woman. I sighed as I doubted fate would give me that.

Hopefully, the blond man would be around for the entire weekend. I wouldn't mind a closer view.

THREE

The hotel got busier as the afternoon went on. I'd considered exploring, but the porch was way too nice and perfect for people watching. So, I spent a couple of hours sitting, watching, occasionally getting caught up in the arrival of someone in costume. I wouldn't have the guts to do that, but it was supercool seeing others doing it.

Sadly, I didn't see the blond man, but the simple afternoon was enjoyable. The chairs were ridiculously comfortable, and I was happy to let the atmosphere relax me into full vacation mode.

I didn't feel bad about not exploring. Having read the schedule, I knew there were tours. One went around the hotel and showed specific places filming had occurred. Another went to various film locations on the island as well as some historic spots. Those would likely be far cooler than any exploring I could do on my own.

Eventually, I pulled myself from the chair so I could grab a shower before dinner. I had the front door open and was about to go inside when the blond man arrived, driving a carriage. He stopped and let a couple out at the front steps.

You'd think I'd never been attracted to a man before. My palms started to sweat, and I had to force my mouth closed since it hung open.

His voice was rich and deep as he offered them restaurant recommendations. *I* wanted a conversation with him about anything.

My mind raced to come up with somewhere I could go. Before I figured it out, I was down the stairs and standing at a respectful distance as the couple finished up their transaction. I couldn't think. Everything was a jumble. I didn't know the island well enough to have a destination.

"Looking for a ride?" It took me a moment to realize the blond man was talking to me. I stared for a moment. His hazel eyes sparkled in the sunlight and even his beard seemed to shimmer. He was the handsomest man I'd ever seen.

"Um, yeah," I stammered, mouth going dry. "Um. I've heard there's, well, some great fudge, and I, um, wanted to get some." I fought the urge to run into the hotel and hide. Tongue-tied was not a good first impression.

His smile was breathtaking. It was like being in the presence of a long-lost friend. My stomach somersaulted, and the flutter of excitement was strong. This was what had been missing from my life with Drake. He'd stopped making me flutter.

"Best fudge in the world, if you ask me. I know just the place. Hop in."

The canopy on this carriage was down so there was an unobstructed view of the landscape, and the driver. Wearing a sweater had been a good choice since it was a bit nippy in the late afternoon.

Since it was only me, I decided to sit behind the driver's seat, hoping we'd talk as he took me to wherever the fudge shop was. As we departed the hotel grounds, I marveled at how easy he made it seem to guide the horses. It was only my second ride in a horse-drawn carriage, but I'd trade this over a regular taxi any day.

I angled sideways so I could see the scenery *and* him. He'd pushed up the sleeves of his jacket and shirt, and, under the fine dusting of hairs, he was lightly tanned, proving just how much time he spent outdoors. The tan was present in his face too. I didn't expect to see that in late October, but I guessed he worked outside enough to maintain a hint of color.

"I take it this is your first time here since you haven't experienced the fudge," he said.

"Just got here a few hours ago." I watched his profile. He looked briefly my way and smiled again.

"You're here for the *Somewhere in Time* event then?"

"Yeah. Finally took the plunge."

"You'll have a great time. They do it up right, immersing people in the film and the island. I learn something new every year from the panel discussions. My dad was sometimes a speaker because he shot a lot of pictures during the filming."

"That's cool. You grew up here?"

"Except for college, I've lived here all my life. Don't really want to be anywhere else."

I relaxed as he spoke. He might be handsome, but he put me at ease. He probably dealt with people so often it came naturally to him just like it did for me in a business setting. Except this didn't feel like business. His ease made me want to be around him more.

"The winters don't drive you away? Chicago's freezing enough. I can't imagine what it's like up here."

"It can get pretty intense, but it's also beautiful. When the lake freezes over and you can go out on the ice, it's fun. Kinda magical."

"Really?"

He looked back at me and gave a nod of his head. "Really."

"Amazing," I said quietly. The idea of a lake as big as the one I'd been on earlier today freezing over was mind-blowing. I'd seen ice in Lake Michigan around Chicago, but I'm sure it wasn't safe to walk on.

"I'm Miles, by the way."

"Jordan. Nice to meet you." I paused before I decided to find out more about him. "I saw you earlier, walking along one of the hotel paths with a horse and a woman. Do you work for the hotel?"

"I'm working with the hotel for the weekend since there are a lot of people who'll want to ride for the tours. My family's owned stables on the island for decades, and we help out the hotel when they have big events like this one."

He worked for himself. There was at least one thing we had in common. I made a mental note to ask him about his business because the more we had to talk about, the more I could be around him.

"That's cool. No wonder you're here all year."

"Yeah, gotta take care of the horses and the property. It'd cost too much to move them for winter. Plus there's something special up here." His voice took on a wistful quality. "People pull together. We're a tight community anyway, but in January and February, it's on us to keep one another entertained, safe. There's only a few hundred of us, and we're kinda one big family."

"It takes a helluva table to feed everyone, though."

He laughed, as I hoped he would. "You'd be amazed how big the potlucks can get."

I'd lived in cities all my life and couldn't imagine living in a place so small and isolated. At least cold didn't turn me off. But, I couldn't wrap my head around living somewhere with so few people.

"Do you offer riding lessons?"

"Of course. I can hook you up if you want. I'm leading one of the location tours for beginning riders. You could do the same thing in a carriage or on a bicycle, but some of the guests want to get out on horses."

"I've never ridden before."

"The tour would be perfect for you. We take time to go over the basics, using the friendliest horses we've got. I'll be leading and some of my staff will be along to help too." He turned back to look at me. "You'd be fine. I promise."

I believed him. I'd pretty much believe anything he said.

"And we're here." He brought the carriage to a stop.

How'd we get here so fast? We stopped in front of Ryba's Fudge Shop. Damn it. I didn't want to be done talking to him.

"Any particular recommendations?" I asked, getting as much time with him as I could.

"Well, you gotta get the chocolate. It's basic, but it's a classic and delicious. I'd recommend the peanut butter too, and the maple pecan is my most favorite. But be careful, it's so easy to overeat the stuff and then regret it."

"I'll keep that in mind." I reached for my wallet. "What do I owe you?"

"I can wait if you'd like a ride back." His hazel eyes drew me in. I'd noticed his eyes before, but with only a few feet between us, they were impossible to ignore.

"That'd be great." I suppressed the urge to yelp in excitement.

"Perfect. I'm going to pull up to the curb and get the horses watered. I'll be ready when you are. Feel free to take your time."

"Thank you," I said, stepping down from the carriage.

Was he flirting? Or were his eyes just doing a number on me? Maybe it'd been too long since anyone had looked at me like that. He was sending mixed messages—comfortable, intense, tentative—that were scrambling my thoughts. My gaydar couldn't decide what to make of Miles either. Usually it was pretty good, but there were no clear signals. Maybe I was too hyped up to read them right.

The smell of the fudge shop was intoxicating with chocolate and other delicious smells vying for my attention. My sweet tooth knew no limits, and my mouth watered, knowing something good was on its way. It'd be easy to buy one of every flavor for the ultimate sampler platter. After I looked through the selections, I went with Miles's recommendations and got a quarter-pound of each. I also picked up a bite-sized piece of the maple pecan.

Each block of fudge came in a cute pink box along with its own plastic knife. The young man that rang me up said it was for easy, on-the-go cutting. Of course, I'd have no shame just picking up the block and taking a bite out of it. I appreciated the idea of civilized fudge distribution, though.

I stepped out of the shop and found Miles next to the carriage. He held a bucket in front of one of the horses while at the same time he stroked the side of the horse's head. It looked like he might be talking quietly to the animals as well. It was a picture-perfect moment, the man and his horses standing on this old-time street. In a sepia tone, the picture could pass for something taken decades ago. I hesitated to pull out my phone and snap the picture, though. It felt like I'd be intruding, so I'd hold it as a mental image instead.

"For you," I said as I approached Miles, holding out the small piece of wrapped fudge.

He set the bucket on the ground in front of the horses, who were content to keep eating.

"You didn't have to do that." He grazed my hand as he took the morsel, and I was sure I'd feel that heat for days to come. He inhaled before unwrapping it. "And my favorite too. Totally unnecessary, but thank you."

The horse closest to Miles snorted and nudged Miles with his head when he popped the fudge into his mouth.

"I think he's jealous he didn't get some."

"He's mad I stopped rubbing him," Miles said, once he'd swallowed the treat. "Wildfire is an attention hog. Aren't you?" He grabbed both sides of the horse's head and gave him a good scratch. "You'd think he was a dog. So, are you going to explore some more, or are you ready to head back?"

"I suppose I should get back. I need to get ready for dinner."

Miles nodded as he climbed up to his perch. "They are sticklers for appearances, but it makes for an elegant dining experience. You'll enjoy it. Even better are the costume dinners once the event starts up."

"I'm looking forward to that." I settled in where I'd been before so our conversation could continue. "Hopefully I have a proper outfit."

"Don't want to be called out like Collier was in the movie, eh?"

"No, I really don't." I laughed. "I figure this crowd's going to be hardcore for period, and I didn't want to take any chances. I suppose I could've gotten a direct copy of the wrong suit from the movie, but I wanted to go for authentic 1912. I'm assured that's what I've got."

"That's what he thought too." Miles turned just enough so his smirk was visible.

"Are you trying to make me nervous about tomorrow?" I immediately thought about the suit and how it looked compared to the ones in the film.

"No, I promise." He sounded regretful. "But there are usually a few people who do show up with clothes that aren't as accurate as they thought. I have the feeling you know what you're doing, though."

"Sounds like you know the movie pretty well."

"I love it. Not only because the island looks so good and that it still brings tourists in, but it's a great love story. I didn't appreciate it when I was younger, but it clicked for me during college."

His phone rang before I could respond, and he apologized that he had to take it.

I adjusted in my seat so I faced the back of the carriage rather than watching him take the call. He appreciated the film for both its economic impact on the island and its love story. That appealed to the business consultant and romantic in me. Just one more thing to draw me to him. Why couldn't I have met him in Chicago?

Miles was agitated, and I felt bad I was hearing it. From his side of the conversation, it sounded like an argument related to the business. Once he'd disconnected, he apologized again.

"It's okay." I adjusted so I could look at him again. "Sometimes things come up."

"I shouldn't have answered it with a passenger, but since I'm the boss, I have to be available."

"I run my own business, so I know how that goes."

He nodded, but this time it was a tight smile rather than the warm and inviting one. Hopefully, I hadn't said something wrong and it was just the call bugging him.

"So will I see you for the riding tour in the morning?" he asked as we pulled, all too soon, into the hotel drive.

"Yes."

I had no choice but to say yes. I wasn't going to give up an opportunity to be around him and hear the stories he'd have.

"Great. We'll meet at the stables at nine thirty, and you'll be back in time for lunch. It's the best way to see everything, I promise."

FOUR

Overnight, I left the French doors open just a crack, which brought cool, crisp, clean air into the room. Perfect weather for burrowing under the covers because it was in the forties. It was the most refreshed I'd woken up in a long time. It was actually a struggle to get up because I was so cozy.

By the time I arrived at the stables, I'd had a lovely light breakfast of eggs, toast, and coffee and checked in for the weekend's activities. There were some people already dressed for the occasion too. I wished I'd splurged on period outfits for the entire weekend, but that seemed extravagant.

Miles was a vision in khaki and green since the various shades worked so well with his eyes and hair. Not to mention how they hung off his working man's physique. Especially the shirt and vest, which showed how pumped his chest was. The definition wasn't visible, but the sheer size of him was well outlined. Again, I struggled not to stare. It was silly to get caught up. I was only on the island for a few days, and Miles had already been clear this was his home.

"You made it," Miles said, smiling at me. "Good morning."

I reached out to shake his hand, even though it wasn't necessary. I wanted to see what kind of grip he had, and I wasn't disappointed. We were about the same height at around five-ten, but he had muscular bulk compared to my workout-as-little-as-possible physique. I wasn't fat per se, but I could stand to lose a few pounds. I felt the weight of all those pounds standing next to Miles's perfection.

"It's a great morning to ride," he said. "Looks like it'll be a group of about a dozen if everyone shows up. If you go on in, Caleb will set you up with Buttercup and show you through the basics."

"Great." I managed to hide my tinge of disappointment that Miles wasn't my teacher. Of course, he was the leader and had to greet people, so I don't know why I expected personal treatment.

Finding Caleb was easy since he was standing next to the stable marked with Buttercup's name. Caleb had me walk the horse outside and then gave me a bunch of instructions for how to work with her—when riding and walking. He also showed me how to mount Buttercup. It wasn't as easy as it looked, at least not for me.

"I swear I'm usually more coordinated." I was embarrassed that I couldn't do it. Caleb, who couldn't have been older than seventeen or eighteen, made it look easy. Not to mention some of the others in the group were already riding their horses around the enclosure.

"It's okay." His tone was encouraging. "Try to keep the momentum going so you get the one foot in and then keep going to swing the other up and over."

Setting up to do it again, I willed myself that this would be the magic time I'd end up in the saddle. Making the push with my right foot, I suddenly felt hands on my butt giving me an extra push. The push came with the slightest of squeezes. Caleb hadn't seemed the type.

"There we go." Miles's voice came from behind. "Now you're up." He came around where I could see him and stroked Buttercup's mane. "Caleb, sometimes you just gotta give people the extra boost."

He clapped Caleb on the shoulder and gave me a wink.

"Yes, sir," Caleb said as Miles went off to check on the others in the party. "Okay, so now you can walk her around. Remember what I said about the...."

I paid half attention to Caleb because the wink and the squeeze I'd gotten from Miles drew my focus. He'd squeezed my ass, and I didn't think that was an accident. He could've lifted me without that extra touch. I liked it because it was playful.

Luckily, Buttercup seemed to know what to do more than I did. She gave me no trouble. I'd caught enough of what Caleb said that I seemed to know the basics, and Buttercup took it from there. We had a successful, albeit slow, trip around the paddock while others were getting ready for the trip.

Miles swung his powerful leg over Wildfire. How had I not noticed how Miles's legs looked in those tight pants, not to mention his ass? If I wasn't around so many people, I might've slapped myself for having those thoughts. I couldn't let myself fall into lust with this man, despite the fact his ass was giving me other things to consider.

"Okay." Miles addressed the group. "We're going to ride out. You'll follow me as we ride on some trails and streets around the island. We'll stop to look at locations as well as some spots that weren't in the film, and there'll be plenty of time to snap pictures. I'll be up front, and we'll have Caleb,

Caitlyn, and Grant with you in case anyone needs help. Sound good?"

Murmurs of yes came from the group, and then we were off. We traveled at a leisurely pace, which gave me time to get used to Buttercup. I fell in with the middle of the pack, and that put some space between Miles and me. He got me flustered, and I didn't want to be that way on the horse. Miles didn't need to get any wrong ideas either, since I'd involuntarily flirt if given the chance.

"Much of the movie was shot on the Grand Hotel's grounds," Miles began as we headed away from the main building. "But, we're going to get started at a place that everyone thinks is on the grounds, but isn't."

We headed out and went north on the western side of the island, along the road I'd seen when I was on the ferry. The hotel stayed to our right and a boardwalk was to the left. It was only a few minutes before I got goose bumps as we approached a small grove of trees just past the end of the boardwalk.

I recognized the place immediately. It was where Richard and Elise met beside the unique heart-shaped tree. Everyone excitedly chattered around me, and for the first time on the trip, I felt alone. I was the only one on this tour who wasn't with someone else, so I had no one to share this moment with. All of this was making me emotional. It might be sappy to get worked up over a tree two actors had stood in front of nearly four decades ago, but I couldn't help it.

We stopped and dismounted to get closer for pictures. I couldn't imagine doing what Richard had done in the movie —approaching a stranger and introducing himself. It was ballsy putting yourself out there like that. Propriety dictated that she rebuff him. Their first meeting wouldn't be their last.

A marker, which was set into a boulder, declared this as *the* meeting spot from the movie. I cleared my head of the romantic fantasy I was having and pulled my phone from my jacket. I snapped a selfie before Miles came up and offered to take a couple of shots from farther away.

"Smile, Jordan. You can't stand in this spot and look all gloomy."

I couldn't be near Miles and not be affected by his energy. I didn't even have to put on a fake smile because his presence wouldn't allow it.

"That's better," he said.

I grabbed some close-up shots of the marker as well as the lake beyond the trees before he called everyone together.

"If you'll pass your phones and cameras over, we'll get pictures of the entire group around the marker. Get in close and stay in place until we snap one for everybody."

We did as we were asked, and once I had my phone back, I went to Buttercup and managed to get in the saddle in a single, unaided try. Luckily, I quelled a victory yell.

"Would you mind snapping a picture of me up here?" I asked Caleb, and he reached up to take my phone. "No one's going to believe I actually did this without proof."

He silently stood back and snapped from a few different angles.

"There you go." He handed the camera back with a smile. "Everything you need to show off your time with Buttercup."

We were out for almost ninety minutes, and I learned a lot about how the movie was shot on the island. Miles had a fun mix of stories—many that could only come from someone whose family lived here during the filming. The island was more beautiful than I'd imagined with its classic architecture in town and the natural beauty all around. From what Miles said, regulations on the island made sure there was little change.

"You're doing pretty good." Miles settled Wildfire in next to Buttercup as we rode back to the stables. "Enjoying yourself?"

I hadn't expected him to drop out of the lead position. I gripped the reins tighter, while trying to make sure I wasn't sending the wrong signals to Buttercup. A runaway horse would create the wrong impression.

"I am. Your stories are great and riding a horse is more fun than I thought it would be."

"Well, you're on one of the best. Buttercup's just about as amenable as they come. Isn't that right, girl?" He leaned over to stoke her neck, and she neighed, clearly agreeing with him.

I decided to talk about safe topics, so I asked about one of the stories he'd told earlier in the tour.

"Your story about watching *Superman* in the same row of the theater as Christopher Reeve was awesome. Do you seriously remember that?"

"I do. I was four, so it's on the edge of my memory, but yeah. He was a nice guy to the island kids. In the scrapbook my dad made, there's a picture he took of me in a Superman T-shirt next to Christopher. He was kneeling so he was on my level, and it looks like I'm about to take off to fly."

"That's awesome," I said. "A helluva a memory, and to have a picture on top of it."

"I wish I'd agreed to show Dad's pictures this year for the convention." Miles furrowed his brow. "I think you'd enjoy them."

Miles's pull on me was fierce, and I forced down my

desire to ask him to get together to see them. We held each other's gazes too long as the horses kept going along the trail.

"I think I would." That was as close to asking him as I could get.

"How long are you in town?"

"Through the hotel's closing ceremony. I thought it'd be cool to take part in that."

"I'll be there too. Maybe we can grab coffee or dinner before you go home, and I can show you some of Dad's collection. Since you're here the extra day, it wouldn't interfere with the weekend activities."

"I don't want to put you out." I offered the chance for him to rescind the offer, while my heart soared that he asked to spend more time with me.

"It's no trouble. It'll be fun to show them to someone I know will appreciate them."

"Okay then. I'd love to."

FIVE

Entering the Grand's dining room Friday evening was like walking into the movie. It was an extreme goose bumps moment, which the day had been filled with. While I'd been here yesterday for dinner and taken in the differences with the color palette and some of the other specifics from the film, coming in to a room full of people dressed in period costumes made it feel like we might all be extras in the dinner scene.

I spotted Melanie, George, and their daughters as I entered, and they waved me over to their table.

"Don't you look handsome," Melanie said as I took a seat.

I'd been in many tuxedos over the years—from prom to weddings to formal dinners. I dressed up enough that I'd even bought a basic black tux so I could stop renting them. What I wore for dinner, I'd found at a vintage clothing shop that specialized in formal wear. I'd been an uber geek talking with the owner about what I was looking for. I'd even brought the movie on my tablet so we could compare clothes. She seemed to enjoy taking me through her stock until we found the perfect suit. With some alterations, it was perfectly tailored, and I felt great in it. I hoped I might find some other event to wear it to because it seemed a shame only to wear it here.

"Thank you, ma'am." I offered a slight bow, which coaxed a laugh out of the girls. "Don't worry, that's just about all of the 1912 manners you'll see."

"Have you had a good time so far?" Melanie asked.

"Very much. I did the horse tour this morning and loved it."

"Awww, Mom, see," Angie said with a pout. "I tell you every year we should do that."

"I'm scared to death of those horses." Melanie looked terrified even talking about it. "A bicycle is much more my speed."

"The horses are gentle," I said. "I've never ridden before and I did just fine. They give you a little training before you go, but I think Buttercup would've taken me around and brought me back with no effort on my part."

"Buttercup?" Cathy giggled. "You rode a horse named Buttercup?"

"I did, and I'd be happy to ride her again."

"Can we, Mom?" the girls asked together.

"We'll see," Melanie relented.

"And we're still on for golf in the morning?" George asked.

"I am. Did you complete the foursome?"

"All it took was leaving word at the front desk, and they had it filled quickly."

"Great. That'll be a good start to the morning."

Dinner was a multicourse feast. The flavors of beef,

garlic, and potatoes were sublime. I didn't know if the food was correct for the period, but it was delicious. The meal's conversation focused on the day's events. I enjoyed hearing what everyone did with their day since it let me in on some things I'd missed while doing other activities.

As dessert was served, a string quartet began to play, and some people took to the dance floor. There were plenty of people dressed in replica costumes from the movie's dinner scene along with many Richard and Elise pairings.

"May I?" George asked as he stood and held a hand out to Melanie.

"Yes, please." He took Melanie's hand as she looked back to the table. "Excuse us."

I gave another nod, and the girls beamed at their parents. George and Melanie looked blissfully happy as they joined the other couples.

As the girls and I ate dessert, I marveled at them. It was hard to believe any teen wanting to come to something like this. During dinner, the girls hadn't even gotten fidgety without their phones. These were the kind of kids I wanted one day.

"Excuse me, sir," a voice whispered into my ear. My pulse quickened as I recognized it. Was he really doing this?

Miles was stunningly handsome, more than any other man in the room. He wore a simple black-and-white tux that showed him off beautifully. Rather than *Somewhere in Time*, this was a fairy tale, and I was the one the prince had come for.

"You look amazing," I said.

"As do you. May I have this dance?"

My gaze darted around the room. There were other gay couples here, but they weren't dancing. It was unusual for me to feel skittish about being out in public. Maybe it was less about what other people would think and more about Miles asking me. It'd been a long time since any one had asked me to dance.

"Yes." My voice didn't hesitate to take the leap while my brain processed what was happening.

The girls' subtle "oohs" were politely quiet. I gave them just a quick glance of stink eye, which made them giggle.

Miles led me out to the floor, and we settled in with the other dancers. I tried subtly to dry my hands inside my pockets so Miles wouldn't be stuck gripping my sweaty palms. Our initial steps were klutzy as we figured out who was leading. I relented since he was the one who'd asked.

"I hope you don't mind my boldness," he said as we settled into the waltz. "I watched you all through dinner, and when the music started, I couldn't stay away."

"I'm glad you did. I've enjoyed getting to know you, and it seems you're a delightful dancer so this is a great addition to the evening."

I thought I might fly apart at the seams. Miles wasn't doing anything in particular, but every fiber of my being was tingling and alive—more alive than it'd been in... longer than I could remember.

We danced and danced. I was the belle of the ball, which was kinda ridiculous, but it was a feeling I couldn't shake. The confident, positive vibe Miles gave off made it hard to feel otherwise.

"You're a good dancer," Miles said.

"My parents wanted to make sure I could hold my own if I was ever in a formal situation. It's served me well about three times in my life."

"I'll have to thank them one day."

"You've clearly had lessons too."

"Sometimes there's not a lot to do up here, so my mom taught my brother and me when we were kids."

It'd been a long time since anyone made my pulse quicken like Miles was. The many lights of the ballroom flickered captivatingly in his eyes while his smile was just enough to trigger the dimple on his left cheek. It was all ridiculously cute.

Across the room, a photographer was taking pictures of the couples dressed up. He had a vintage box camera on a wooden tripod, and he held up a flash lamp to illuminate his subjects.

"Wow." The flash kept catching my eye. "That's hardcore old-school photography."

Miles laughed. "Yes and no." He continued to keep us gracefully dancing. "He built that rig just for this event. There's a digital camera tucked inside that box. He emails the images out later, and for a fee, he'll even manipulate it so it looks like it was from 1912."

"Okay, not as cool as I'd thought, but still a great way to keep up the authenticity."

"Wanna get a picture? Capture the moment?"

"Sure." It'd be great to have a memento of this swoon-worthy moment with Miles.

We walked across the dining room, and Melanie caught my eye and smiled. I grinned right back at her.

We got into the short queue and waited for our turn. As we got to the head of the line, the photographer popped out from under the hood attached to the back of the camera.

"Hey, Miles," the man said. "Didn't know you were here."

"I got a free dinner since we're helping out more this year, and I haven't pulled out this suit in a few years so I decided to give it a whirl." He looked over to me. "Jordan, this is Luke, one of my best and oldest friends and the man who put this camera setup together."

"Nice to meet you." I shook his hand as Luke stepped from behind the camera a bit more. "Miles told me how this works. Very cool setup."

"Thanks," Luke said. "Shall we get your picture?"

We got into place and Luke went back under the hood. He told us to do a couple simple poses, one of which was Miles's arm around me just above my waist. I was sure this would become my favorite picture from the weekend.

"Thanks, Luke." Miles and I stepped out so the next couple could take our place. "I'll catch up with you next week."

"Sounds good." Luke peeked out from behind the cloth. "Good to meet you, Jordan." And then his head disappeared again.

"I've enjoyed this," Miles said as we took our time walking back to my table. "Unfortunately, I've got to say good night. It's an early morning tomorrow to get things ready for the tours."

I hated to let him go, but I understood too.

"Thank you for a delightful time. I enjoyed starting and ending the day with you, especially the dance."

"Perhaps we'll get to do it again sometime."

"I hope so."

In princely fashion, he gave me a slight bow as he left me at my chair. "Good night, Jordan."

"Good night," I said, smiling at him.

I watched him go, and just before he left the room, he turned and gave me a wink and a smile.

"Are you just going to stand there or sit down and talk to us?" Melanie asked. I had no idea how long I'd been swooning in Miles's wake.

"Sorry." I took my seat.

"Don't be sorry. I'd say you had a great time."

"I did."

As the five of us finished dessert, it was hard for me to stay focused since most of my senses were still in full swoon mode.

SIX

Spending the morning with George and two other guys was the right way to start Saturday.

It was relaxing and a much-needed distraction from the dreams I'd had about a certain blond man who'd swept me off my feet. I still wasn't sure what to make of it. Miles had been a perfect gentleman, which made him all the more appealing. There were no expectations. It was simply a wonderful evening. The only thing that would've made it better was to have started earlier and had dinner together.

The course was beautiful and the guys were a good time. George worked for a public relations firm and the other two worked in finance. The conversation was around business, which was easy, or sports, and I had plenty of opinions about the Chicago-based teams.

I lost myself in the beauty too. Like so much of the island, the golf course had a magic and wonder of its own. The back nine was incredible. It was known as the Woods, and it was in the middle of the island, surrounded by forest. To get there, you rode in a carriage for fifteen minutes through the wooded landscape. Not that the front or Grand

Nine wasn't spectacular on its own, situated across the street from the hotel. Sometimes I had to be prodded to take my turn because I was all too happy to turn off my mind and watch nature.

George was the best golfer among us, but I hung in with the other two as we kept trading second place. Coming into the sixteenth hole, I was hanging on to second by a stroke. As I placed my ball to tee off, a staffer on a bicycle approached.

"Yes?"

"There's a call for you." The young man handed me a cell phone. "The gentleman said it's important."

That's odd. No one knew I was out here, at least none who would call.

"Thank you." I took the phone and found Drake's mobile number on the display. "I'm sorry," I said to the trio. "Play through and I'll catch up."

Drake had better have a very good reason for not leaving a message. I stepped a few feet away from the group while the guy who'd brought the phone retreated to his bike.

I took a deep breath so I'd start the conversation calm. "Hello?"

"Good God, that took forever. Did they have to get the phone to you in the middle of the lake or something?"

"Is everything okay?" I was genuinely concerned. Even though Drake was being a pest, to have the phone brought to me, it could be a real emergency or something.

"You haven't exactly been calling me back, and since I've got arrangements to make, I decided to make sure the phone landed in your hand. There's a conference in Aspen that I'm going to, and I know you love Aspen and this would be a good thing for us to both go to."

I should've known. It was always business. Frankly, I

was surprised he remembered I liked Aspen. The three times we went, he'd barely skied or done anything with me. Instead, he had spent his time trying to make business contacts.

"Did you talk to Alberto?" My grip tightened on the phone. "He can decide on conference attendances while I'm on vacation."

"You should be the one who goes to represent your firm."

"It's *our* firm and you know that. Why'd you really call?"

Alberto and I worked with Drake and his firm often, sharing clients and making referrals. We'd found the corporate synergy early when Drake and I had started going out. It might be time to revisit that, though, if he was going to try to use it to try to lure me back to him.

"What do you mean? This conference has some great speakers lined up. It'd be a chance to network beyond Chicago, and that could grow your business. Plus, well, *Aspen*. We could, maybe, start over."

"You're kidding, right? The mere fact you're using business to try to woo me is one of the reasons we broke up. You're consumed by business twenty-four seven, and that's not what I want my life to be. Send the information on the conference. Alberto and I will review this week. I'm going back to my game now."

"Jordan, don't you—"

I disconnected, refusing to let him finish. Did he really expect I'd go to a conference as a date? He didn't even ask how I was doing or if I was having a good time. It was all about business, and *maybe* getting back together with me. There was no romance in that, at least not like I desired.

Drake didn't seem to get why we broke up. However,

the more he went on with the campaign to try to get me back, the surer I was that he wasn't for me. Of course, the guy who made me swoon for the first time in a long while also lived on an island hundreds of miles away. None of my previous relationships had made me feel like Miles had during the time we'd spent together last night. Yes, each one of those had started with a spark, and there were moments of passion, but the pull Miles had....

"Will that be all, sir?" asked the young man who'd brought out the phone, pulling me out of my thoughts.

"Yes, thank you." I took a ten from my wallet to give to him, hoping the hotel's no-tipping policy didn't extend to the golf course. He shouldn't have had to run out here for that ridiculous interruption, so I wanted him tipped.

"Thank you, sir." He pocketed the phone and the cash before walking quickly back to his transportation.

"Everything okay?" George asked as I rejoined the group just as he was about to send the ball flying.

"Yeah, just a call that wasn't as urgent as the caller thought it was."

George shook his head. "I know those all too well." He took a moment to set up and then swing. He dropped his ball on the green. "You're up." He looked to me.

The final two holes were good, even though I finished in third place. Our foursome had brunch in the clubhouse before we all traded business cards. It'd been a great time, even with the disruption. It was a delightful morning with new friends and exactly what I needed to keep from replaying last night on a loop.

I headed back to the hotel solo since George was meeting Melanie and the girls in town. I hadn't seen Miles, which wasn't surprising since he had tours to do.

There were two days left on this trip, and I didn't want

to leave, which was unusual. Even if I'm enjoying myself, I'm typically ready to go home before the vacation even hits the halfway point. While I liked traveling and all that goes with it, I also liked being at home and in my routine. I wasn't missing the routine here, though. If anything, I enjoyed having no routine. Maybe that was the fresh air and retro environment working on me.

As I arrived on the hotel's porch, I pulled my cell phone and dialed Alberto.

"Jordan! How's the past treating you?"

"The event is awesome. The golf's great. You'd love playing here. Just wait until you see the pictures I've got. I've got two days left, and I'm kinda dreading having to leave. It's like I'm in a storybook, and it's kinda perfect."

"Why not stay for a few more days? You barely take time off as it is. Or work from up there, if you want. It's all good as far as I'm concerned."

I knew he'd say that, but a guilty feeling always rose up if I wasn't in the office when I was supposed to be. Alberto was in and out, and I never worried about what he was doing. He was right, though; there was no reason I couldn't work from here—or even extend the vacation.

"Thanks, Alberto. As always, you're great."

"Glad I could point you in the right direction. Now go enjoy yourself."

"Yes, sir."

"Attaboy," Alberto said. "Later, my friend."

I had just enough time to grab a shower and get to the first of the afternoon panel discussions, including one I really wanted to hear about how *Somewhere in Time* might play if it were made today.

Instead of going to my room, though, I detoured to the front desk. I'd made up my mind about one thing.

"How can I help you, Mr. Monroe?" It was the same clerk who'd checked me in.

"I'd like to stay on the island longer than I'd planned. I know the Grand closes Monday. Can you recommend other accommodations for at least a week?"

"Absolutely. If you'd like, we could make arrangements for you."

"That would be great. Wherever you think would be best."

"I'll see to it we have something booked for you by this evening. Check back then, and the details will be ready."

"Thank you."

I wasn't exactly sure what I was going to do with the week, but at least I'd have a roof over my head.

SEVEN

Once the afternoon panels were done, it was time to get back outside. I laughed a little at myself. I'd never been one to be outside all that much since I was a kid. Here, the outside beckoned like a siren song. The break before dinner was a perfect chance to go for a walk and think.

I wished I trusted myself enough to get a horse, but I was far from confident in riding solo. My meanderings took me to the boardwalk near the hotel. The lake was soothing as the waves lapped at the shore. The lakefront in Chicago was nice, but with all the buildings and people, the feeling was nowhere near the same. Here, the nature and quaintness encouraged relaxation.

Settling on a bench that looked out over the water, I watched as the sun made its way toward the horizon. As was the case a lot over the past few hours, Miles drifted into my thoughts. Why couldn't he live in Chicago? Of course, if he was in Chicago, he wouldn't be the man he was—the one who works with horses, knows the best place to get fudge, and loves the same movie I do.

Perhaps I could use part of the coming week to find out

more about him. If nothing else, *Somewhere in Time* proved you have to take a leap sometimes. Richard gave up everything to go back in time to meet Elise. Nothing as drastic as time travel would happen if I saw Miles again.

The light played across the water as the sun gradually changed position. Periodically, horses clopped by on the street behind me while birds chirped in the trees. I couldn't remember the last time I'd been so peaceful. Being away from the city, and on my own, made me realize how much hustle there was in my life.

Suddenly, Miles's voice was in the distance, and he didn't sound happy. I couldn't make out everything he was saying, but it was a heated discussion. Hopefully, I could sit here, since I was off the road, and he'd ride by so there wouldn't need to be an awkward moment.

"You realize this could be the end of our family business, right?" he asked.

The soft clip-clop of his horse was all I heard for a few moments.

"I bought you out because it was the right thing to do. Can't you reinvest some of that money to help clean up your mistakes?"

He was right behind me.

"You may have left, but I still live here. It's not my fault you got bored. I would've taken over everything and you know it."

I willed myself to become one with the bench as the horse stopped.

"I gotta go."

I held my breath, hoping he'd nudge the horse into moving. Silence prevailed. Maybe Miles was considering the conversation. Maybe he had a way to make horses go stealth. Maybe he was staring at the back of my head.

"How much did you hear?"

Option three was right.

I pivoted on the bench to look at him atop Wildfire. Of course, Miles looked great in a red plaid shirt and blue jeans along with the denim jacket I'd first seen him in. What I didn't like were the worry lines around his eyes, or the way his forehead was deeply furrowed.

"Enough." There was no reason for me to lie. "Anything I can to do help?"

"Not unless you've got a way to make my brother stop being a self-obsessed ass."

I shrugged. "'Fraid I don't have a fix for that."

"Well, I'm sorry I disturbed you. I should get going, but hopefully I'll see you later."

Before Wildfire could even get a couple of steps, I got up and approached. He pulled back on Wildfire's reins, and the animal obediently stopped.

"Sounded like you're having business problems." I approached Wildfire so I could rub his nose. "Maybe I *could* help with that?"

"I'm not sure anyone can." Miles tensed in the saddle.

"Business strategy is what I do." I looked up at him. "I've never worked with a stable, but I'm happy to offer any guidance if I can."

His sigh sounded like a breath he'd held for years.

"Honestly, it'd be good to talk to someone who doesn't live here. Trying to keep it under wraps, to keep the gossip down, isn't easy. Luckily, Mr. Walker at the bank maintains discretion."

"Tight cash flow?"

"That's part of it." The tension in his voice implied there was a lot more to the story. "You really think you could help?"

"Maybe. Whether I can or can't, I'll certainly keep your confidence."

Miles dismounted, and the horse gave a sound of protest while cocking his head to look at his rider.

"It's okay, boy. I got something for you." He pulled an apple from his jacket pocket, which the horse eagerly snatched. "See, it's all good."

The smile Miles had for the horse was unburdened and reminded me of the one I'd received from him just yesterday. He talked quietly to the animal as he led him to a tree to tie him up.

"You sure you want to hear this? You're on vacation after all."

"Tell me." I gestured back to the bench.

"The short version," he began, "is that when my parents retired five years ago, they offered the business to Nate and me. I wanted it. I'd always wanted it. I was the one who loved every minute of working with my parents and the animals. Nate never liked it. He'd complain about every chore there was to do."

He kicked at the ground with the toe of his boot as his gaze darted around. He'd look at me for a moment and then look elsewhere. I kept my focus on him as any attentive listener would.

"I majored in equine facility management to be ready to take over. Nate partied through school and barely scraped by with a communications degree. When Mom and Dad decided they were done with winter, they asked what we wanted. I said I'd take whatever Nate didn't want. Surprisingly, he said he wanted his fair share."

I didn't interrupt, even though I had an idea where this was going. If he wanted to talk, I'd listen to every word.

"My mom was furious because Nate had never shown

an interest. Dad, however, was thrilled that both his sons wanted a part of the business. The decision was to split the locations between us. I got the original, and Nate got the annex. He did some hair-brained expansions and renovations, but in less than two years, he got bored. Decided living here wasn't for him."

He gazed out over the lake, looking like his pride took a huge hit laying everything out.

"I made the huge mistake of buying him out because I wanted to keep the family business together. My business was successful—not anything to boast about, but it did well. He'd left more of a mess than I initially realized, and I haven't been able to dig out."

"How bad?" I asked when he didn't continue.

"It's likely I'll lose both stables at the end of the year."

"Can your parents help?"

"They've offered." He stared off at the horizon. "But I don't want to take away their nest egg. They've tried pressuring Nate to help clean up his mess, but these days, he's more interested in fast cars than horses."

"Do you have everything documented? I could review it to see if you've got options that might've been missed."

He nodded. "Yeah. I've got all the records, and I sorted that out earlier this year. It's my fault. I was too quick to buy Nate out so he'd stop whining. I should've let his half go rather than end up here."

"It gets complicated when family's involved. I've seen it in large and small businesses. Let's get together, and you can take me through everything."

I felt bad for him and wanted desperately to help. I wasn't sure I could. It depended on what I found in the paperwork. I was good at helping small businesses, but sometimes things were too far gone.

He finally looked back at me, and his eyes tugged on my heart. "I can't intrude. You've got the last day of the con tomorrow, closing ceremonies the next day, and then you head home."

"Actually, I'm staying through next week." He cocked one eyebrow up, and I shrugged. "I like it here, so I decided to stay around a little longer."

A weak smile formed, with no dimples triggered. At least it was better than the frown we'd started the conversation with. "Then we can definitely find time for me to show you those pictures and maybe hang out some more."

"I'd love that." I turned his direction and sat cross-legged on the bench so I could face him. "Maybe you can show me more of this cool place you live too."

The smile got bigger and that zinged me with happiness. "That can be arranged for sure." He looked back at Wildfire. "I really should get a move on. I've got a few things to do before the costume competition tonight. See you there?"

We both stood and walked toward Wildfire.

"Yes. Not missing that."

He gave me the briefest of hugs, so fast I could barely reciprocate.

"We'll grab a drink for sure then."

I said goodbye and watched as he rode Wildfire up the street.

EIGHT

"You do this every year?" I asked as I worked with Miles and some others to clear the rocking chairs off the porch of the Grand as part of its closing day after the con finished.

"Every year since I was ten. The only closings I've missed were when I was in college and couldn't get away from classes."

We had a rhythm down of grabbing a rocking chair, taking them in, and returning for another. We stayed close to each other so we could talk.

"It's a real community effort between the residents and guests." We were headed toward yet another pair of chairs. "I've never seen anything like it."

"For the families that've lived here for generations, like mine, it's a tradition."

Miles was in a sweatshirt because the late October air was, of course, nippy. I imagined what it might be like to see him in less so his biceps and triceps were visible as he lifted the large chairs. It would've been a great time to manifest X-ray vision.

"Where'd you go to college?" I kept the conversation on the up and up while my mind undressed him. He'd mentioned he learned how to run the stable, and I'd been curious what that meant.

"Lake Erie College down in Painesville. I learned a lot from my folks, but I wanted to get the formal education as well so I'd know all angles. Lake Erie has a lot of related programs, and it's close to home. I've been thinking lately that I should've taken more straight-up business classes, though."

"Try to stop beating yourself up. It doesn't help. Knowledge doesn't always prevent bad choices."

We'd dug into his situation last night over drinks. We went out after the final costume competition, which he helped judge. I was glad I hadn't participated. It was amazing some of the outfits that were put together. There'd been multiple versions of Elise and Richard, of course. Incidental characters—some of whom I didn't recognize even as much as I've seen the film—were also represented.

While we enjoyed scotch neat—it was cool we had scotch in common—he gave me the longer version of his situation. He also gave me a couple of binders full of papers, most of which I'd sifted through before I went to bed. He was right—there was a lot of trouble. He could sue his brother and win, based on what wasn't disclosed before the sale. But, since it was a friendly deal, contracts hadn't been drawn up. Cash had been paid and ownership transferred. As Miles told me upfront, he'd failed the due diligence he would've done with any other business deal.

"What are you up to the rest of the day?" Miles asked as we closed in on the end of the chair project.

"Gotta make some calls. Even though I'm staying up here, there's still some work to do."

"After you finish and I close up for the day, do you want to have dinner?" He quickly added, "Burgers and beer at the best place on the island."

"I'd love to." I had no hesitation. It was a pretty sure thing I'd say yes to whatever he asked. "A perfect way to start off a new week."

"Great," he said. "I'll pick you up, and we can walk over."

Once the chairs were stowed, we helped wrap up some other tasks and then gathered for the ceremony. The president of the hotel rang the closing bell, officially marking the end of the season. It was very formal and seemed out of place in the twenty-first century. That's what made it so cool.

After taking my time walking downtown with Miles, I went to my new room at one of the island's year-round inns. I was no sooner in the room than Drake called. His name on the display was just about the last thing I wanted to see. I answered it before I could stop myself.

"Hello," I said, as if I didn't recognize the number.

"Hey, Jordan, it's Drake. I just got off the phone with Alberto, and he said you weren't coming into the office this week. Is everything okay?"

Where the hell was this coming from?

"It's great." I took the perky route since he was. Besides, I *was* great, and I wasn't going to let this call taint that. "I've taken on a client up here, so I'm staying for the week and making a working vacation out of it."

"What?" The upbeat Drake who'd started the call was gone. "You said you were coming back. I wanted to set up a meeting with you for a potential new client for both of us. You have to get back here for it."

"Alberto can be there in person, and I'll attend by phone or video. Just let me—"

"You know that's not the same, Jordan." He spoke as if he were scolding a child. "In person is the way deals get done. We do a deal that's good for both firms, and then we all go celebrate. Maybe you and I can get some time together too. Talk about where we went wrong? Get that out of the way before we go to Aspen."

He missed our routine and maybe the status afforded him of having a boyfriend who owned a growing business. I seriously doubted he missed *me*.

"Drake, you know why I broke it off. I'm not the guy for you." I walked over to the window to look out at Market Street. I didn't want to rehash this stuff, but I guessed he hadn't heard it the first time. "I wanted more than the facade of a happy couple but feeling like a business partner. I want romance and to feel like I'm loved. And I want to give that back to someone."

"You and that fucking movie. This isn't 1832, or whatever, Jordan. It doesn't work that way."

I knew otherwise. The couples I'd met over the weekend, like George and Melanie, only fortified my feelings. I wasn't around enough of the right people. The more I thought about it, the more I realized most of the people I hung out with tended to drift through relationships, which wasn't what I wanted. I needed to connect more with my happily coupled friends. That would be something that changed when I got home.

"Make the appointment with Alberto, and I'll be there virtually. It's the best I can do since I've already made commitments here."

"Fine." Drake was pissed that he wasn't getting what he wanted. "I'll email you."

It was a relief that he just hung up rather than dragging the conversation out. I crossed the small room and dropped into the desk chair so I could open one of Miles's binders. Alberto and I had an appointment to talk about the stables.

"Sorry about that," Alberto answered just before voice mail would've kicked in. "The earbuds were tangled."

"No worries." My mood was already bouncing back from his jovial voice. "How's Monday going?"

He ran through details on what had happened so far, including his review of the conference that had prompted Drake's golf-interrupting call.

"Seems like you're having a good day." He shifted topics once we'd addressed the business concerns. "I saw you moving chairs on Facebook and have to say that was the oddest thing I've seen in a while."

I laughed with him. "It was a lot of fun."

"It looked like you were enjoying yourself. You know I only like cardio, so if they needed me to run around the building I'd do that. Lifting furniture, not so much."

It occurred to me that Drake had said nothing of the picture even though he must've seen it. Alberto was on Facebook far less than Drake, and if Alberto caught it, Drake surely had. It made me wonder if he had a meeting to set up, or if the call was a response to what I'd been up to this morning.

"So I've got a project I want to look into," I said as an overture before giving Alberto the high-level summary of Miles's situation.

"Yikes. It's sad that family would hide something like that."

"Right? Do you think we'd have any short-term investors who might help turn it around under our guidance?"

I'd worked with Alberto long enough that I could easily imagine the look on his face as he considered his answer. "We've never dealt with this kind of business before. I'm not sure we can leverage anyone in our current investor network."

"I was hoping you'd think of someone I hadn't." I was disappointed but not surprised. "I ran through a lot of options and came up cold."

"What's the bank's position?"

"There's at least one party circling, hoping for a foreclosure. The bank is willing to let it lapse even though his family's done business there for decades."

"Ouch. They must think a good deal is going to come if they're turning their back on a local customer like that."

"Unless it's another local customer. I'm going to see if I can find out more." I paused before I continued, since I was headed into uncharted territory for our business. "I might want to use some of our discretionary fund for this. I'll do more research before I decide, though."

"Okay." Alberto's hesitancy was clear. "We usually use that when we're working with local Chicago businesses. It's not explicitly written in our business plan that we do that, but I want to make sure we're aware of the change in the status quo."

"I know. I've got some ideas, though, on how to make it work for Miles and not be a liability for us."

"I trust you. Just gotta have my business hat on."

"I'd be disappointed if you didn't."

"Can I ask why the interest in this?"

Oh, man. I wasn't sure I wanted to admit this to Alberto, even though he wouldn't judge. Since I was having a hard time with the relationship status myself, I wasn't sure if anyone else should be in on my topsy-turvy thought processes.

"I kinda like Miles."

"Oh my God." Alberto laughed heartily. "You sound like a schoolboy with a major crush."

From some people, that might've offended me, but with Alberto, I saw the humor. "Yeah, I might be."

"Does this mean...?"

"I don't know." I stopped him before he could ask more. "We've been hanging out a lot. He asked me to dance with him the other night and—"

"Wait. What? You're holding out on me."

"Oops." I suddenly felt a little guilty. "Sorry, man." I recapped the dancing and some of the other time we'd spent. "I love every minute we're together."

"Good for you, man. No wonder you wanted to stay up there. I expect you to keep me better informed on the situation. Is that understood?"

His gentle chiding made me laugh. "Understood."

He shifted back to business. "Send me your research summary when you're done, and I'll see if I'm missing some possibilities on my side."

"Thanks. You'll have that today."

NINE

"A personal tour. I'm honored," I said as I got off the bicycle I used to get to Miles's stables. He was outside, waiting with Wildfire and Buttercup saddled and ready to go.

I'd been in my room, putting the finishing touches on a presentation I was set to give with Alberto the next day, when Miles's call came in. He invited me out for a sunset ride, and I felt just like the giddy schoolboy Alberto had accused me of being.

I went right up to Buttercup and stroked the side of her head. Miles handed me an apple to give her as well. It seemed like she recognized me as she sort of nuzzled my hand. Although, maybe she was this way with anyone who fed her. I was less nervous around her since I knew what to expect this time out.

"I'm glad you said yes." Miles did a final check on the horses to make sure we were good to go. "It's been a long day of winter prep. Once the Grand closes, we get ready for the slow season. Moving chairs has nothing on getting this place buttoned up."

It was obvious by his enthusiastic talk and smile that he enjoyed what he did, even if he did look a little tired.

"When does winter usually kick in here? So far, it just seems like good, crisp fall air. Maybe slightly colder than Chicago."

Miles chuckled. "It's really like anywhere else, and it does vary. It's at its coldest usually late January and February. If the ice bridge is gonna form, it's usually February."

"Ice bridge? Seriously?"

"Oh yeah. Between here and St. Ignace the lake can freeze up and you can walk across or take a snowmobile."

"I can't imagine."

The enthusiasm Miles had for the cold had a warming effect on me. Even with the issues he was having, he stayed upbeat most of the time, at least from what I saw. It was an impressive quality.

"It takes at least a week of zero or below, and with no wind, to create the three or so miles of walkable ice."

"Be awesome to see that sometime." I took Buttercup's reins from Miles.

"I'd love to show you." He spoke softly and met my gaze briefly before mounting Wildfire. There was longing in his eyes, and I diverted my attention to Buttercup as shyness welled up in me. It was quick, but I wasn't used to someone looking at me that way. "Shall we?" he asked in his regular voice.

I managed to mount Buttercup, with decent form, on my first try. While I wasn't anxious to ride, I was more than a little nervous—or, maybe, excited—being around Miles. He definitely made me jittery, and I just couldn't figure out all the emotions behind it.

We headed out, and the route was recognizable because

it followed the start of the locations tour. Even though I'd been here a few days, it was still odd to be on the streets with no cars. It was far less crowded than over the weekend too.

It didn't take us long to turn on to Lake Shore Drive, the island's perimeter road. It was a bit after six and the sun was heading down, brilliantly orange in the clear sky and reflected in a kaleidoscope of reds and yellows on Lake Huron. We passed the *Somewhere in Time* tree, and it wasn't much after that we were past town so there were mostly trees on my right and shore to the left. The more I was in secluded places like this, the more I liked it.

We rode side by side, with Miles to my left.

"This is so incredible," I said. "I know I've been here before, but the whole thing is still unbelievable—from being right on the shore to riding a horse instead of being in a car."

"I thought you'd like this. We'll stop in a couple of minutes and watch the sun drop behind the bridge."

The few people who passed us, headed back the way we'd come, said hello. Most called out to Miles by name, and all had a friendly greeting. Miles was always quick with the hello, sometimes giving it first. It took me some time to get into it. I'd gotten used to giving nods to the people I passed in town, but it still felt weird greeting practically everyone. It just didn't happen in the city, so it was against my instincts.

"We're going to pull off to the right here." Miles pointed to a spot after we'd ridden in comfortable silence for a few minutes.

There was a pullout that was planked over, like the boardwalk near the Grand. As we came to a stop, a marker caught my eye. This was called Devil's Kitchen. After we dismounted, Miles tied up the horses while I read the plaque.

"So you've brought us to a place where the spirits are said to capture and eat victims who wander too close. Charming," I said.

"You can imagine the horrors that a child could have venturing too close to this place." He took one of the saddlebags off Wildfire.

"You're not planning me as a sacrifice or something, are you?"

"Halloween's over. Maybe next year." He winked at me. "Actually, this is a perfect spot to watch that." He pointed to the west, across the lake.

My breath caught, seeing the colors that played across the sky and water in an amazing display as the sun touched the top of the bridge. I'd watched a couple of island sunsets, but this one was spectacular because of our vantage point.

Miles jerked his head toward the shoreline, and I followed across the street. Just off the pavement, there were rocks that led down to the water's edge. He'd clearly been here before because he went directly to a rock formation that was taller than the rest.

"The perfect seating for the best show on the island."

It was ideal. The size of the rock bench, for lack of a better word, kept us close with shoulders and legs touching. I had to remind myself, though, that we were just friends and sometimes friends sat close. Still, I liked the contact far more than I probably should've.

"And I brought refreshments." He pulled things from the saddlebag. "Coffee and milk-chocolate fudge."

He handed me the thermos and set the pink fudge box on the ground in front of us. He also produced two mugs, so

I opened the coffee and poured as he held them. I quickly closed the thermos and set it aside so I could take a mug.

"Cheers," he said, and we clanked our mugs together.

"You really know how to stage a sunset." I took a drink. "And you know how to make a cup of coffee too."

"I do, but in this case, it's from Ryba's. It's a one-stop shop for all things decadent. Somehow, they manage to mix the fudge into the coffee. I've been an addict since I was fourteen. Dad got me hooked on it."

"I think I'll be one too." I drank as Miles carved fudge off the block. "It's dangerous I know about this because it'd be too easy to have it every day."

We sat quietly, eating, drinking, and watching the sun drop behind the bridge. Periodically, there'd be horses or bikes on the road behind us, but mostly the only sound came from the gentle waves just a few feet from us. This was just one more thing to love about the island—and Miles. My insides were all aflutter, and I fought against quaking on the outside.

"One of the best light shows I've ever seen," I said as the sun went out of sight.

"How about we take in a sunrise?" Miles asked. "We could meet up about seven and ride over to Arch Rock."

Was he trying to woo me? Dancing, horse rides, sunsets, and now sunrises were pushing all the romance buttons. Did that even make sense? Five hundred miles separated our lives. Although, Richard and Elise lived nearly seventy *years* apart, and they still found each other.

"It'd be a great way to kick off a day." I reached for the fudge box to slice off another piece. "I'll buy breakfast after."

"It's a date." My eyes had easily adjusted as darkness

fell, so I didn't miss the uncomfortable look on his face. "Well, not really a date, of course."

"Of course." I looked back toward the bridge, which was now lit up. "What're you up to the rest of the evening?" I went for a less awkward topic. I guess he'd considered the practicality of the distance between us too.

"Put these horses to bed and get myself to sleep too. I'm usually an early riser."

"Same here. Always have been. It's tough when I've got meetings or whatever at night because my body just wants to be in bed by nine." Miles nodded, and after a quiet moment, I continued. "Thanks for bringing me out here. It was incredible."

"You're welcome. There's something about here. I think it's the best place on the island to watch sunsets. I come here often because it clears my head, especially these days. My dad used to do it too. Maybe we can do it again."

"Yes."

I fought against my instincts, which screamed at me to nuzzle closer to him. Instead, we sat in comfortable silence until we'd drunk the last of the coffee.

"We should probably get going," he said. "I'll send you home with the fudge."

"I might just bring it along as a breakfast appetizer." I took the box and stuffed it in my jacket pocket.

"That works. Unless you eat it as a midnight snack."

"Very possible." I stood and offered him a hand up. "The last batch I had called to me every time I saw the boxes. You sure it won't be safer with you?"

"I can get fudge anytime. You're the visitor; you should definitely have it."

"I'm not gonna argue."

We laughed as we returned to the horses, who seemed

happy to see us. Miles pulled carrots from the saddlebag he'd left on Wildfire and handed me some. Buttercup eagerly chomped them down as I scratched near her ears. Miles also handed me two Velcro reflector strips.

"Strap those on your biceps so you can be seen," he said.

As I did that, he turned on a small light that was hanging at about chest level on each horse. The white light coming from them lit up the street for several feet.

"Clever," I said as I mounted Buttercup.

"Safety first." He secured Wildfire's bags before mounting.

We rode back to the stables, talking occasionally but mostly just taking in the night.

TEN

"Do you know Cal Larchmont?" I asked Miles when I got to his office in the afternoon. We'd had a great morning with the sunrise and breakfast. Afterward, I'd had a productive time getting some work done, which included digging further into his business.

"Yeah," he said as we shook hands and half hugged as he welcomed me into his office. The space was functional but cozy with lots of customer pictures and thank-you notes displayed on a large corkboard along one wall. "Why do you ask? And why do you even know that name?"

We'd shared the half hug a few times this week, and I enjoyed them and the tingles that shot through me in the aftermath. The more we touched, though, the more I wanted full contact. Restraint was getting more difficult. The logical part of my mind seemed to have been strangled by the carefree romantic.

"I've been looking into who's trying to get this place and why the bank would rather go that route than help you keep your family business. There's a high probability he's the one circling."

Miles dropped into his desk chair and rubbed his hand across his forehead.

"I should've guessed it. Larchmont's wanted property here for years. There are strict guidelines on development. With so much of the island being a state park and the entire thing classified as a national historic landmark, it's not easy to get a foothold here. Two or three years ago, he lost out on a couple of larger properties, which are now undergoing huge renovations to bring in additional tourists. He approached my dad about selling when word got around he was retiring. I think he's bought two homes that he's made vacation rentals."

I sat in the chair across the desk from him. His distressed expression wasn't one I liked. Larchmont scared him. More than anything, I wanted to make this right.

"Yeah." I pulled out my tablet so I could take notes. "He's bought four actually, one from a seller directly and three that were in foreclosure."

His expression fell a little more.

"The deals were probably made before it became public," I continued. "No doubt the former owners were happy to avoid the public embarrassment of having that kind of for-sale sign on their property. I'm surprised he didn't try to buy out Nate."

"He couldn't. When we got the business, the contracts were designed to help keep it in the family. Nate had to give me first refusal on it, and vice versa. As long as our parents are living, they have final right of refusal."

I nodded. "There's no guarantee that Larchmont's the one, but from the poking around we've done, it looks likely. Given that he's paid cash and full market value for properties, it's no wonder the bank would be okay if this all went to foreclosure."

"*We've* done?"

"My business partner and I. We're digging around, as we would for any client."

"But I'm not a client."

"No, you're more. You're a friend." I fought the urge to take his hand and squeeze it to reassure him. "And helping businesses is what we do."

"Even ones this small?"

"We've helped smaller." I flipped some pages in one of the binders he'd loaned me and held up a page to make my point. "You've got a sound business plan, and before you took on Nate's debt, you were solid."

A smile crept across his face. "Do you always make the worst situations sound okay?"

I closed the binder and set it with the others, glad I could brighten his mood with some facts.

"Business is hard enough without worrying. You already think about your livelihood, your employees, and so on. I always try to emphasize good where I can, but I won't sugarcoat either."

He stood, picked up the binders from the desk, and moved them back to the bookcase behind him. "How do I fix it?"

"I don't want to sound glib, but the easiest way to make all this go away is pay off the debt before the end of the year. I'm guessing that's not possible even though the tourist season exceeded expectations."

We both knew the situation so he simply shook his head.

"We could try to put together some investors for you."

"How's that work?"

"We find people in our network who'd be interested with the goal to get enough cash to cover the debt. The investment group would co-own the business, and in this arrangement, you'd pay off as fast or slow as you can. The investors would also take a percentage of your profits until payoff. That percentage wouldn't count against your principal."

"What keeps the investors from deciding to foreclose?"

"As long as you're running a viable business per the terms of the contract, they couldn't. We'd work with you to form the business plan that makes the most sense."

"What's in it for them?"

"People have various reasons for investing."

His brow creased as he considered what I'd said. "I don't know. It feels like I'd be going from one debt to another."

"I hope you know I wouldn't recommend something to you that I didn't think was the way to go."

He looked conflicted as he started to talk and then stopped himself several times. He finally sat back in his chair and looked confused. I knew it was hard. All he wanted to do was run his family's stable, teach people how to ride, lead tours, and such. He knew how to do it under normal circumstances, but this was an exception. What I wanted to do was punch his brother for putting him into this situation.

"What?" He sat forward, looking at me as I barely contained a chuckle at my thoughts.

I couldn't stay silent and ended up snorting as I giggled. "I was thinking about finding Nate and beating him up."

"Hmmmm. I've never had a protector before."

The look Miles leveled in my direction was smoldering, unlike anything I'd seen from him, even during the lushly romantic dance, which I admit to playing back in my head many times since that night. Heat and exhilaration radiated from my chest as I enjoyed being the one he looked at.

I stood, leaned over the desk, grabbed Miles, and pulled him closer to me so I could plant my lips on his. He grunted at the initial touch, but he wasted no time kissing me back. The scratchy feel of his mustache and beard against my face were extra pinpricks of pleasure on top of the kiss.

My tongue traced his lips while his tongue darted out to meet mine. We explored each other tentatively—as if we couldn't decide how far to go. Perhaps we knew we'd already gone too far.

Without warning, Miles put one knee up on the desk and slid himself closer to me. Papers scattered as he shoved them aside. The mug holding his pencils and pens crashed to the floor when the desk's contents were further disrupted by Miles bringing his other leg up so he was kneeling on the desktop. His hands landed on my shoulders, pulling us together.

Miles took charge, ignoring the mess we were making. He pushed his tongue deep into my mouth while I flashed back to our dance. What would it have been like to be kissed like this on the dance floor? He slipped a hand around my head while my grip tightened on the back of his. We dueled over who was in more control of the kiss. The back and forth was hot, and more than ever, I wanted to know what sex with this man would be like. There was no stopping now.

At least until there were two sharp knocks on the door, followed by, "Boss?"

We froze, looking at each other while our lips were still together. His expression was playful, and for a moment, I thought he was going to ignore the interruption.

"Yeah?" He called out, breaking our kiss.

"The Milners are here for their tour."

"Thanks, Caleb. Get the horses ready, and I'll be out in about five minutes."

"Sure thing."

"That was close," I whispered.

"Nah. They respect a closed door." He rested his forehead against mine. "What did we just do?" He sounded unsure.

"As the one that started it, I can say I have no regrets."

To emphasize my point, I kissed him again. My heart soared as he kissed back. It was quick, though, because we didn't need to get fired up again. He had a tour to do after all.

"Can we go to dinner tonight?" He crawled off the desk. "And let's just call it what it is. A date."

"I'd like that," I said quickly. I didn't want him to sense any hesitation, even though there was a little. I didn't want to mess this up.

"Great." The excitement was palpable in his voice. "I'll pick you up as soon as this tour's done, probably around six thirty. I'll give you a call when I'm on my way over."

He straightened the papers on his desk while I knelt to pick up the writing implements scattered on the floor, between shards of green and blue ceramic.

"Didn't mean to cause a mess."

"If you're gonna kiss me like that, you can make all the mess you want. And you can leave that, I'll get it later."

I left the mug's remains on the floor but dropped the pens and pencils on the desk.

"I should let you get going. The Milners are waiting."

He grinned and nodded. "Yes, they are. Come on then."

He came around the desk as I put my tablet back in my messenger bag. Once I slung it over my shoulder, he wrapped his arm around my waist and guided us toward the door. Before he opened it, I got one more kiss.

"I'll see you tonight."

I nodded as he opened the door. We stepped into the main stable, and just outside, Caleb stood with three horses along with the Milners. There was a sting of jealousy seeing that one of the horses was Buttercup. I'd had no idea that I'd forged that sort of attachment to the animal. Or maybe I was jealous because I wasn't the one going out with Miles, Wildfire, and Buttercup.

I needed to get myself on the riding schedule.

Miles raised an eyebrow and nodded to me before he headed off.

"Sorry for the delay," he said as he crossed the stable, and I headed out the main people entrance, as Miles called it. I had some things I wanted to check on, based on the business talk we'd had. That would keep me occupied so I wouldn't watch the clock.

ELEVEN

Dinner was wonderful. We talked endlessly about growing up. I told Miles about my exploits as a peewee hockey player, a career that ended after I'd sprained my ankle. Miles had hockey tales too, including playing pickup on the ice bridge in the dead of winter. He talked passionately about forming a bond with the horses and family business in middle school. Meanwhile, I related my stories of business exploits as a kid. I'd been determined to have the best lawn-mowing business when I was fourteen. In college, I'd created a food-delivery business.

Best of all, the night ended with a kiss. When he brought me back to my hotel, he gave me the sweetest kiss that I was all too happy to return. I went to my room deliriously happy. And, while I wanted to have sex with Miles, I was glad we weren't moving that fast. The goodnight kiss was the right cap for the evening.

By the time lunch rolled around the next day, I'd already sent six business reviews to Alberto. To celebrate, I invited Miles to eat with me.

"This is becoming a thing." Miles dropped into the seat

across from me in the booth. "We're eating together more often than not. People may talk."

"You mean they're not already?"

He laughed, and I loved being the reason for it. There was no doubt now that I was falling for Miles. I just wasn't sure what that meant in the long term, and for now, I didn't care.

"You know small towns?" he asked.

"I know your family goes back a ways here, and I'm sure everyone keeps an eye on you. Plus, I've gotten extra smiles and nods on the street these past couple of days. I'm thinking people approve."

"Well, you're here past end of season, which already makes you extra special. But, yeah, people are talking."

My face warmed in embarrassment, even though I already suspected I was the subject of town gossip.

"Don't worry. It's good talk. There was even a message from my mom when I got home last night because the news reached her, and she wanted details."

"No," I said in shock as my face went from warm to blazing hot. "She did not."

"Scout's honor." Miles raised the three fingers in the proper salute.

"Oh my God." I dropped my head into my hands, mortified it'd gone that far.

"It's okay." He pulled one of my hands toward him and wrapped it in his strong, callused grip that I'd already come to love. I wondered often what those hands would feel like exploring my naked body. "What I went through with my last guy is pretty well-known, so folks are watchin' out for me."

"Hey, Miles." A waitress came up to our table. "What can I get you guys?"

"Tina, this is Jordan." I gave a nod, and Miles let go of my hand.

"I've seen you around. Nice to finally meet you."

"You trust me?" Miles pierced me with those hazel eyes. I'd have said yes anyway, but his look gave me little choice.

"Of course."

"Okay, we'll go with burgers, medium. Tell Marty to use the maple bacon and throw an onion ring and pepper jack on it. Oh, the special toasted bun too."

"Fries?" Tina asked.

"Of course." Miles made it sound like she was crazy to ask the question.

"Drink?"

He looked at me and raised an eyebrow.

"Up to you." He'd done great so far, so I saw no reason to stop him from completing the order.

"Gotta go with root beer then."

"You got it." Tina leaned in and whispered near my ear, "You're in for the best burger ever."

A grin broke out across my face. She bounced up and headed behind the counter to put the order in.

"And here I thought it was just a normal lunch," I said.

The diner's door opened with such force the bells sounded like they were hanging on for dear life. My back was to the door so I couldn't see who came in making such a racket, but Miles made a face of scorn.

"What?" I asked so I wouldn't have to turn around.

"You should see this guy. Fancy-looking suit, fancy overcoat. Don't usually see that in the middle of the day here. I mean he's dressed beyond what the Grand requires for dinner. And he's looking around like he's meeting someone."

"Jordan." My blood went cold. "There you are."

I turned to find Drake coming toward the table.

"Fuck me," I said softly as I turned back to Miles.

"What kind of godforsaken place is this? I have to take a carriage or bicycle from the airport? How do you deal with that?"

He stopped at the edge of the table, looking at me and not acknowledging Miles. Everyone eyed him, diners and staff alike. I'd have been okay if the bench swallowed me up so I didn't have to deal with this.

"How the hell did you find me here?"

"Since you didn't tell me where you were staying—and, again, you weren't answering your phone—I had my assistant waste his time calling around until he found it." He made it clear to everyone sitting within earshot how much he'd been inconvenienced. "So I came up here. Of course, you weren't in your room, but as I was walking around, I saw you in the window here." We stared at each other for a moment. "Are you going to scoot over?" he asked coolly after I didn't move or speak.

"No." I sounded far calmer than I felt. "I'm having lunch. Drake, this is—"

"Come on," he interrupted before I could introduce Miles. "You need to at least talk to me since I managed to get here."

"No. I kinda don't. Whatever you had to say could've been done on the phone or waited until I got back to Chicago."

"That's days away."

He looked at me expectantly. One of the looks he often used on people to get what he wanted. I let him use it on me at times when it was just easier to relent. I didn't want to make a scene, but I wasn't giving in either.

"Just go. Get back on the plane and go home. We'll talk

next week." I shot an apologetic look at Miles. "Now if you'll excuse me, I'm in the middle of lunch."

"You don't get to brush me off."

"This fancy man bothering you?" Tina had just the right amount of distain in her voice. It was difficult not to smile at her. I had the feeling she'd throw him out if I asked her to.

"Yes." I pushed out of the booth so fast Drake had to dodge out of my way. I looked to Miles and Tina. "Will you make sure my lunch stays warm, please?"

"You got it," she said, as if I was one of her regulars.

I snatched Drake's hand and dragged him from the diner. The more he tried to take his hand back, the more my grip tightened. At least outside his yelling wouldn't interrupt people's meals. Of course, diners would no doubt watch our show through the window.

"Why, Drake? What made you think coming here was the right thing to do?"

"Is that man why you're staying here?"

"*Miles* is my client." Drake didn't need to know there was more going on than that.

"Is Alberto okay with you being up here so long?"

"That's not your concern. Should I be asking if your boss is okay with you being here in the middle of the week?"

I felt bad going for the jugular. It was always a sticking point for Drake that he was *only* an executive vice president in his firm, and I was copresident and cofounder in mine. I outranked him and had no one to answer to except my equal partner and myself.

"Everything okay, Jordan?" It was Mrs. Tanner, the owner of the inn I was staying at. She parked her bike on the rack next to us.

"Yes, ma'am, just a slight disagreement. Sorry to have disturbed you."

"Oh, it's no bother." She waved her hand in front of her face as if clearing a bad smell. "Just wanted to make sure one of my favorite guests wasn't having trouble."

"It's none of your concern even if he is." Drake sneered.

Mrs. Tanner didn't even flinch. I suspected she saw all kinds at the inn. With one more look of concern, she went into the diner.

"You need to go." I hoped the firmer I sounded the more the message would get through to him.

"I'm sorry." He was calmer but still exasperated. "It's just.... How am I supposed to make up with you if you're up here?"

He reached out and ran his hand over my flannel shirtsleeve. I didn't want him touching me, but I knew if I pulled back, he'd start yelling again. I took a deep breath, letting the smell of the clean air, mixed with a bit of fudge, help me keep my emotions in check.

"What can I do to fix this?"

"Nothing. It's been months now, Drake. You need to let us go."

"Come on, we were together long enough we have to at least try."

He stepped closer and tried to kiss me. This time I backed away. After the kisses I'd had from Miles, I didn't want one of his, which in no way compared to Miles's.

"No."

As if he hadn't heard me, he continued forward and managed to get his lips on mine before I shoved him back.

"I said no!" My anger unleashed.

"Why are you making this so hard?" He matched my pissed off tone.

The bells on the diner door jingled, but my attention stayed on Drake—at least until a hand came down on my shoulder. I looked to my left and found Miles.

"Everything okay out here?" he asked.

"No. It isn't okay." Drake was barely hanging on to his patience. "Why can't everyone mind their own business?"

"Drake was just leaving," I said.

"Not until we talk."

"I think he said you were leaving." Miles stepped up on Drake. He was imposing, and I was grateful I'd never brought this out in him. "You're not from around here, so I tried to give you the benefit of the doubt. But you were rude to Mrs. Tanner and to Jordan. I think you should be on your way."

The wheels were spinning in Drake's head. He wasn't often at a loss for words, and it frustrated him when he was. Apparently, Miles was more than he was ready to handle.

"We just need to talk," Drake sputtered.

Miles looked to me.

"Not right now we don't," I said. "He just needs to go back to the airport."

"That I can help with." Miles stepped out into the street for a moment and I saw why. "Caleb?" He flagged down the carriage.

Caleb pulled to the curb on the opposite side of the street.

"Yeah, boss?" the young man shouted over.

"Can you do a pickup?"

"Sure can. Just did a drop at the ferry."

"Perfect. Mr...." Miles looked to me for the missing word.

"Billings," I added, drawing a flash of anger from Drake.

"Mr. Billings needs to get to the airport." Miles swung

back around to Drake. "There's a ride for you, on the house. He'll get you to the airport so you can be on your way with no more bother."

Drake and I stared each other down. It felt like the world stopped until he eventually broke the stare and walked away.

"Did you catch that, Caleb? It's no charge for our friend here."

"Got it. I'll be back to the stable as soon as I'm done."

Drake fumbled his way into the passenger area, continuing to stare at me. If he was trying for a guilt trip, it didn't work.

Miles and I watched until the carriage was out of sight.

"Who the hell was that?" Miles turned his full attention on me. He wasn't happy. "And why was he trying to kiss you?"

"That was my ex."

I didn't know what else to say. How much detail would Miles even want?

Miles's look was skeptical. "That looked more like a lover's spat."

I sighed and managed to keep looking at Miles rather than away. "He's got this weird idea we should get back together. I tried to fix things for so long before I broke it off. I've no idea why he's making these overtures now."

He nodded. "I wish you'd told me about him."

"I would've when we got to *that* talk. It's not like I know about your exes."

"Point taken," he said, smile returning.

Tina knocked on the diner window nearest us and motioned for us to come back inside. The confrontation made me hungrier, so I was even more ready for that burger.

"Glad that's over with," Tina said as we returned to our

table. "I wasn't sure how much longer Miles's jealousy was going to be contained. I'll get your lunch."

"I wasn't jealous," Miles called after her. "I wasn't," he added, quieter, to me.

"Yes, you were," Tina said as she put plates in front of us. She leaned in closer to us and whispered, "Miles Colter, don't make me take a poll of the people in here. They saw exactly what I saw."

Miles studied his food intensely, moving fries around the plate. "Was not."

He sounded like a child who knew he'd done something wrong but was sticking to his story. It was sweet and just another signal that this guy was special. Was he as special as Elise was to Richard? Would I do something crazy to be with him—like travel back in time? Or try a long-distance relationship?

Tina laughed softly. "Whatever you say, sweetie." She squeezed Miles's shoulder. "Let me know if you guys need anything."

We shared a smile before she moved a couple of tables down.

"He's an ass." Miles dressed his burger while I busied myself putting mine together too.

"Yeah, although that was a new level of ass. I'm sorry you got pulled into it."

"'S okay. I suspected you had it, but I thought adding backup would help make him get outta here faster."

"Worked like a charm. And I liked you in the protector role."

He grinned in an *aw-shucks* way that was too cute for words.

"So was he always like that with you?" He got the question out between bites.

"He pushes to get what he wants. Though he was being more adamant than usual just now. He doesn't usually mind a scene either. He believes it gives him the upper hand. Sometimes, I admit, I'd go along to get him to shut up, but I wasn't having it today."

"I thought he might hit you once you backed up from his kiss."

"Feeling was mutual on that one." I chuckled. "I was ready to clobber him. I wish he'd thrown a punch. I would've definitely ended that fight."

"As long as we're talking exes, my last boyfriend was eighteen months ago. He'd moved to the island thinking it was the perfect place to work on his sculptures. We were together over a year, but as his second winter approached, he decided he didn't want this much isolation and cold. He bailed and went to New Mexico for the desert."

"From one extreme to another," I said.

Miles nodded. "He asked if I'd go with him, which I appreciated. But this is my home. I can't imagine being anywhere else. Of course, when I retire, maybe I'll move like my folks did. But I don't see that happening anytime soon. And now we've got the ex talk out of the way."

There was also no doubt on how he felt about this place. I was going to have to think about if this was going to be a long-distance thing, or would it be just a few vacation dates? Was he having similar thoughts?

TWELVE

"Have you started taking drugs?" Alberto asked out of the blue while we were talking business after lunch.

"Maybe, a drug called Miles."

With the phone at my ear, I spun around in my room's desk chair. I was, possibly, a little too giddy for my own good. Maybe I was reading too much into how lunch ended. While I didn't know what the future was, it seemed like there could actually be one.

"I see. I'm guessing there's no twelve-step program for that. How does this play out when you come home?"

A valid question and one I'd thought about a lot in the past couple of days. My reality was the longer I stayed here, the more I wanted to be here even though my life was in Chicago.

"I don't know." I sighed as Alberto groaned in response. "We're avoiding that talk. Can I take a pass from you on it too?"

"Sure." I recognized Alberto's soothing voice as the one he used when he's trying to soften bad news.

"Let's get on to the meeting we're supposed to have."

"All right," he said. "You're not going to like this. Among the investors who tend to work with businesses the size of Miles's, we don't have any takers. I even hit up some of our more eccentric investors and couldn't get a bite."

I wasn't surprised, but I was still disappointed. "Thanks for trying."

"Of course." Alberto sounded apologetic even though he had no reason to.

"You've seen all the information. What do you think about taking on a percentage through the discretionary fund?"

"I'd be okay going twenty-five percent." Alberto paused, and I envisioned the wheels spinning in his head. "Maybe as high as thirty-five depending on the profit percentage because I'd want to replenish the fund as quickly as possible."

"Reasonable."

"But where does the rest of it come from? Even if we go in for the full thirty-five, there's more than a hundred thousand dollars outstanding."

"I'll cover it."

"Jordan, I get that you like this guy, but that's a significant amount of money." Alberto was understandably shocked. "For a single investor to put that much up in this kind of business is something we'd never recommend."

"I know. I'm not our regular investor client either. I believe in the business, not just from the research, but I trust the guy behind it too."

"Well, if you're willing to stake your personal cash, I'll authorize thirty percent to come from the fund with standard terms."

"I'll sign on for that. Thanks, Alberto."

"Are you sure you want to mix business and pleasure like this?"

"He's not going to know the business side."

"What do you mean? He knows we're looking into it."

"Yeah, he knows we're trying to put together investors. He doesn't need to know that either the company or I invested."

"Is that wise? Keeping that big a secret?"

"He's got a stubborn streak. I'm not sure he'll take our help anyway. I don't think it needs to be complicated by knowing who the exact players are."

"Okay. I'll roll with it."

"But you don't like it." I stated the obvious, but I wanted to acknowledge that I knew it.

"I just don't think it'll end well. You're trying to save his business, which is great, but you're also starting a relationship. It seems like a bad idea to mix the two. Not to mention deceiving him at the same time."

"I'll think it through again."

"Good." He was still holding back. "You know I only want happiness for you, right?"

"Always. And what's best for the company."

"The company won't get hurt by this. You might, though."

"Am I about to fuck everything up?" I moved from the chair to the window.

"I hope not. I don't know, man. My track record with boyfriends isn't great, so I don't have a lot of advice to offer. I just don't think you want to leave such a large secret on the table."

"I'll really think about it. I'm gonna get to work on the contract for this and get the cash I need liquidated. I'll also get you the responses you need on the rest of the prospects we talked about."

"Perfect. Later, Jordan."

I pocketed my phone and looked out over the quiet street. Alberto made an excellent point, but I didn't want Miles declining the help. He had a solid business; I knew that in my heart, or I wouldn't be involving my company to help save it. Even if I was blinded because I liked Miles, Alberto would've never allowed it to get in front of our investors if it was a bad move.

I couldn't decide what the butterflies in my stomach were about—hiding this from Miles, trying to start a relationship with him, or simply dreading that I had to go home in a few days.

Going home. That was the elephant in the room. It was only going to get bigger and more unruly the closer we got to my departure day.

The phone rang and pulled me out of the thoughts.

Miles! My butterflies scattered at seeing his name on the screen. I was so in over my head with this guy—and I loved it, despite the questions. I wasn't used to feeling as happy as I'd been over the past few days. I thought I'd been in good spirits since the split with Drake, but this was a new, more intense glee. The downside was if it ended, the crash was going to be horrible.

"Hey!" I said, connecting the call.

"Hey, yourself. What're you up to?"

"Getting some work done. You?"

"Winter prep continues, but I'm actually headed out to give a riding lesson shortly. I'm calling because I just ran into Luke on the street, and he wants to take us for a drink tonight."

"Sure."

"Great." Miles sounded super excited about this. "His wife just went down to Detroit to visit her sister. So, he's solo, and he wanted to get to know you better. You game?"

It was time for the friend test. I was game for that.

"Wish my bestie was here so we could get vetted at the same time. Sure, let's find out what Luke thinks of me."

"He's gonna love you, I have no doubt."

Miles gave me the details before he headed off for the lesson. I had four and a half hours to psych myself up to impress his best friend.

THIRTEEN

"Luke's great," I said, sitting across from Miles at his desk the following afternoon. "I'm glad you have someone like him. Everyone needs a solid best friend, and I know it's weird, but it always makes me sad when people don't. It's important to have the one you can always call up to share the good and, even more important, the bad."

"Yeah." Miles pulled a bottle of whiskey from his desk. "He's listened to me about this business stuff since it went down. He wanted to throw me a fundraiser, even tried to get me to set up some internet thing to raise money. I just didn't want that many people in my business. I'm still a little uncomfortable I've shared with you as much as I have."

Even more reason why I shouldn't tell him I'm the primary investor.

He produced two glasses from the same drawer and set them alongside the bottle. "A little something to celebrate with."

"I'm glad I was in a position to help. It's going to be

much easier for you to pay off everything under this plan rather than the bank's terms."

"It's gonna be great for the staff too. I've been unusually quiet about what's going to happen in the off-season, and now it'll be business as usual. Reduction of hours, yes, but not out of work."

I pulled the paperwork from my messenger bag and walked Miles through the terms. He was about to receive a check, made out to the bank, to clear the debt. It also laid out terms for repayment, the profit sharing, and other legalities. Finally, I got to the part about who the contact at the firm would be, and he stopped me.

"I don't get to work with you?" He questioned why Alberto was his contact.

"I'm too close to you. Alberto and I agree it'd be better if you dealt with him. It ensures the relationship we have doesn't cloud the business."

"I guess that makes sense." He sounded disappointed, which pulled on my guilt a little more.

I tried to ease his hesitation. "I'll always be there, and I'm happy to be involved, but it's the right thing for Alberto to manage this. If you and I end up—" I sighed, dreading the thought. "I don't know, hating each other, your business interests need to be protected."

"Okay."

He grabbed my hand and briefly squeezed it. Some of my tension evaporated as he gave me a nod and a smile.

I read through a few more things and handed over the paperwork that I'd already signed. Alberto would sign it once it arrived in the office, making it official.

"You can have your lawyer go over it, or you can just sign it. That choice is yours. Alberto and I want you to feel completely comfortable with the agreement."

"I trust you. And, thankfully, you've written this in pretty clear language that I actually understand."

He grabbed a pen from a new mug, which was farther from the edge, out of harm's way. Was he anticipating another desktop outburst? I certainly wouldn't have minded.

He signed everything, and we traded the paperwork for the check that he'd give to the bank to clear all the debt.

Miles came around the desk, and what started as a handshake turned into a hug. "Thanks, Jordan. I appreciate that you believe I can turn this around and get your investors paid back."

"You're welcome. Now, let's get that to the bank." I stood, eager to see him put this issue behind him. He didn't move. "What? Something wrong?"

"No." He added a shy smile.

I sat back in the chair, and he grabbed my hand again. The energy passing from him was intense, and it radiated through my body all the way down to my toes. I quaked as my pulse quickened.

"I know we haven't talked about this, and I want to get it in the open. I know we live hundreds of miles apart and that I haven't done a long-distance thing with other guys. But I want to give it a go with you."

His gaze pierced my soul with a look that took my breath away. I hadn't seen this side from Miles, and for a moment, I couldn't find my voice.

"Let's do it," I finally said, my voice cracking.

Miles smiled broadly, and I knew this was right. It had to be.

"Just know that I'm in this with my eyes wide open. If nothing else, I think we can be good friends. If the relationship thing falls apart, we stay friends and laugh about what went wrong later."

Wow. I had no idea he'd thought it through that much.

"All right. Eyes wide open it is." This was scary but thrilling. "Let's just make sure we talk to each other, okay? The more we communicate, the less likely either of us gets hurt."

He nodded, and the excited look on his face elated me even while there were pangs of guilt because of what I was hiding from him.

"I'm going to get this to the bank." He held up the check. "I'll pick you up at six for a celebration." We left his office and headed outside to our bicycles.

"Should I bring anything or dress a certain way?"

"Nope. Just be ready at six; that's all you need to do."

"I look forward to it."

We kissed before we got on the bikes. The ride was silent except for parting words as he turned to go to the bank and I continued on to the inn.

The thoughts swirling in my head made me anxious, even though I was delighted at the prospect of what was to come. The difficulties of long-distance dating… not wanting anyone to get hurt… desperately wanting to get Miles in bed… eager to see what he had planned for the celebration…. It was a loud cacophony that wouldn't stop. At the eye of the storm, though, was the shining knowledge that he wanted to go for it.

I hoped I was worth it for Miles.

FOURTEEN

I SPENT an hour trying to decide what to wear. Luckily, I'd been able to do laundry at the inn, since I hadn't packed to stay so long. I almost went on an impromptu shopping trip, but I wasn't sure that'd make the choice any easier. Part of the problem was Miles hadn't told me what we were doing, so I had no context to help me choose. All he'd said was that he'd pick me up at six.

I was still reeling from the talk in his office that we were going to make a go of this—distance be damned. I was so anxious that I quaked periodically, and the butterflies in my stomach were making me just a touch nauseous. I couldn't remember the last time I'd been this worked up. It was a sign that I was head over heels for Miles; otherwise, I wouldn't be feeling this way.

I tried on dark blue jeans, which made my butt look good, along with a crisp white shirt and a black blazer that was extra heavy to cut the chill. Looking at my ensemble in the mirror, I still wasn't sure it was right. The shirt hung off me nicely and the coat looked good over it, but it didn't seem right. It was almost too formal.

I got rid of the shirt and coat and looked at the clothes strewn across the room. I settled on a sky-blue pullover. It was a favorite of mine for when I wanted to feel cozy on chilly nights. I slipped it over my head and, giving myself the once-over again, decided this was it. The color worked well for me. It looked good with the jeans and with the blazer over it.

I wished Mrs. Tanner, who was in the parlor adjacent to the lobby, good evening and went out onto the porch to wait. Right at six, a carriage pulled up. I came down the steps just as Caleb climbed down from the driver's seat.

Odd. I thought Miles was picking me up.

Shit. Maybe he'd changed his mind. But he'd still tell me himself, or at least I thought he would.

"Good evening, Mr. Monroe," Caleb said. He was dressed in the same fancy attire I'd first seen Miles in. "Mr. Colter asked me to pick you up."

He motioned to the seating area. Caleb was never this formal.

"I'll have you to your destination in about five minutes, Mr. Monroe. Please make yourself comfortable and let me know if you need anything."

He gave me a brief nod before he returned to the front of the carriage.

"You can call me Jordan." I tried to make things more casual. "We have met after all."

"No, sir. Not this evening."

Miles was up to something and I loved it. Sure, getting picked up by him would've been nice, but this was sort of fancy. I'd never been chauffeured to a date in a horse-drawn carriage before. It was going to be an amazing night, especially if I could relax.

I hadn't meandered too much into the residential areas

of the island. I'd seen a small portion on the movie location tour since there were a couple of island houses where filming had taken place. We'd left Cadotte Avenue and were in what must be the heart of where most of the residents lived. These were beautiful homes—all well maintained.

"Do you live nearby, Caleb?"

"Yes, sir. My family lives on Fourth. We'll pass it on the left shortly."

The view was amazing, even though the trees were mostly bare. It was magical riding in the carriage, and it'd be more so if Miles were here. I waved to people who passed on bicycles or horses, and even to a couple who were on their porch and greeted me first. It felt silly waving from a carriage—I wasn't royalty after all. On the other hand, everyone was being friendly, so it would be rude not to wave or say hello.

Eventually, Caleb made a left into a driveway. The house was a splendid two stories with dormers on the second floor—an architectural feature I loved. Red brick ran along the lower part of the house and, above that, was light gray paint and white trim. The major pop of color was the bright red door, which matched some of the bricks. There was space for a garden and it, along with the flowerbeds, was cleared for winter.

It was beautiful. I imagined it was even more spectacular in the green of summer and the color of early fall. The house looked welcoming, and some goose bumps spread over my arms. It was similar to how I felt pulling up at the Grand, except this made me even giddier because this had to be Miles's home.

As if on cue, Miles stepped out on the porch and was a handsome sight. He also wore jeans, so I'd chosen correctly.

He'd gone with a dark long-sleeved shirt. We were a good match.

Damn. I wished I'd known I was coming to his house, though. I'd have brought something. Somewhere my mother was flinching because I'd come to someone's home without a gift.

Caleb brought the carriage parallel to the porch, and I climbed out.

"It's good to see you," Miles said as he came down the stairs and wrapped me in a hug. It was no half hug either. It was a full-out, both-arms-around-me hug.

"You too. It was pretty amazing getting picked up. I felt like Cinderella." I looked over my shoulder to Caleb. "Thanks for the ride."

"My pleasure, sir," he said.

"You've taught him well. He wouldn't break the formality even when I told him he could."

"Good." Miles offered an impish grin. "Thanks for playing chauffeur tonight. You can relax now."

"Thanks, boss." He became the Caleb I recognized. "Glad I could help out. You two have a good night."

"'Night, Caleb."

"Bye," I added as he guided the horse and buggy back toward the street. "That was an impressive way to start," I said once Caleb was out of sight.

"Not too over the top?"

"Maybe, but I liked it."

I leaned in and kissed him, which he seemed happy and eager to return. The kiss lasted just long enough to leave me wanting more.

"Come on in." He took my hand and led me through the front door.

Unlike the outside, which seemed to stay true to its

original design, inside was a well-thought-out mix of classic and modern. The moldings and woodwork were set against modern amenities like a large-screen TV over the fireplace.

"This is beautiful." I inhaled the aroma of fresh baked bread, which made my mouth water.

"My mom gets most of the credit. I haven't changed it much since I took over the house because it feels like home. There are things she hates, like the big TV. But she was outnumbered by the men in the house."

I chuckled. "I think a lot of moms lose those battles."

"Come on into the kitchen. Dinner's almost ready."

"Oh my, it smells amazing." As we got closer to the kitchen, the full aroma hit me. There was the scent of garlic and basil and just a hint of chocolate.

The kitchen was tricked out with modern stainless steel and gadgets. But there was also a feeling of homey tradition here with the cabinetry and other fixtures that looked as though they were original to the house.

"This is partly how we won about the TV. We argued the living room could have the TV since the kitchen had all this."

"I'd say your family knew exactly what it wanted."

On the stovetop was the bread, mostly hidden away under a light orange tea towel. There was also a sauce on the stove, which I suspected was where the garlic and basil smell was coming from. There was a pot of boiling pasta too. I couldn't place the chocolate anywhere. Maybe I wasn't smelling right. Not that it mattered because everything I saw looked scrumptious.

"You're quite the chef from the looks of it." I watched as Miles stepped over to the stove to stir the sauce.

"I do okay. My mom made sure her boys knew how to

cook to help woo whoever we wanted. Take a seat and help yourself to some wine."

I sat at the island he'd gestured to and poured a glass of Riesling.

"Thanks. Shall I top yours off?"

"Sure."

I served and asked, "What's on the menu, Chef Miles?"

"For your enjoyment this evening, we've got a light salad of greens with homemade lemon vinaigrette. The main course is pasta with grilled chicken and pesto along with a medley of sautéed squash from my own harvest. For dessert, a chocolate cobbler that is a specialty of the house."

"Sounds delicious."

Miles had his back to me, working at the stove. He had a gracefulness as he moved—even if it was simply stirring a pot—that couldn't be ignored. The best, though, was when he opened the oven and bent over to check what was inside. His butt looked scrumptious. I wasn't going to rush things, but I wouldn't mind if I got a look inside those pants tonight.

"Is there anything I can do to help?" I snapped back to reality and remembered my manners.

"Set the table? And I'll get everything into serving dishes."

"Deal."

I scooped up the plates he'd already gotten out along with other things as he directed me. The dining room was the one room that looked untouched from the past with light blue floral wallpaper, white wainscoting at the base of the room, chair rail, and crown molding. The furniture was definitely antique.

"This is an amazing spread," I said once we were seated

with filled plates. "I don't think I'd have the guts to cook for someone on a first date."

"Well, you've been on the island long enough that you've probably eaten everywhere at least once. This was someplace you hadn't been. And I've been cooking long enough that it doesn't freak me out to do it for someone new."

"And it's very good."

"Cheers, and thank you for everything." Miles's eyes reflected the light around the room. He lifted his wine glass, and I did the same.

"Cheers, and you're welcome." Our glasses gently pinged.

"I consider myself one lucky man for meeting you," Miles said after we drank. "Not only have you saved my business, but I haven't met anyone I wanted to make my boyfriend in a long time."

Wow. He threw that out there calmly. I loved hearing it, but it didn't do anything for my earlier jitters.

"I'm lucky too. This island's been magical, showing me what's missing in my life. Helping you with your business was nothing compared to how happy I am that we're doing this."

Miles's expression was hard to read, and I suspected I knew why. Sunday was fast approaching, and while we'd agreed to try long distance, we hadn't talked about what that involved.

"After dinner, I'd love a tour of the rest of the house." I moved to a much safer topic. "It's quite something."

"It's a lot of house for one person, but, like the stables, I don't want to let it go."

"Nate didn't want the house?"

Miles shrugged. "If he did, he never mentioned it. He

stays here when he's on the island, but that hasn't happened in months. Do you have siblings?"

"Nope. Just me. Raised in a run-of-the-mill suburb of Chicago. My parents still live in the house I grew up in, except my room's become Mom's craft room."

He softly laughed. "Plenty of room for crafting here. There's four bedrooms upstairs, plus a workshop out back."

"How do you keep all this up with just you?"

"Someone comes in once a week to clean. I'm pretty tidy anyway, but I don't want dust all over the rooms I don't use much."

I nodded. "So Nate just decided to up and leave even though he took on one of the stables?"

I might have been treading on something that wasn't my business, but I was curious.

"Dad and I've talked about it. We're sure Nate thought he was doing the right thing. But a girl who was visiting turned his head. He decided to sell and move. To his credit, he's still with the girl."

"That's something, I suppose. Does it ever get old, living in such an isolated place?"

"It's home. It's always felt like home. And I love what I do. The tourist season's exciting because you meet so many different people. The off-season's great because there's a little more rest. And, the community is really tight, which I like."

"You don't mind freezing up here?"

"I've heard about Chicago when the wind is whipping off the lake. I'm sure we both sometimes wish we lived in Florida."

"You're right about that. That desire to bolt usually crops up in February."

"So Chicago's where it's all at for you?"

"Except for school, it's the only place I've ever lived. I've never thought about anywhere else. Never had a reason to." I locked eyes with Miles as I spoke, and I could've stayed in that moment forever because his gaze was enthralling.

For a moment, neither of us knew where to go with conversation. We focused on eating in a comfortable silence. It was one of the best meals I'd shared with anyone.

FIFTEEN

"Wow," I said as Miles snapped on the lights, illuminating the back porch.

"This was Mom and Dad's hideaway. A lot of parents make it the master bedroom, but for them, it was to sit outside, hold hands, and talk about the day. I need to put the storm windows up, but the heater will do just fine for tonight."

The porch was screened in and hundreds, if not thousands, of tiny white lights along the ceiling provided soft illumination. There were a couple of chairs and a small couch on one side and a small round table with chairs on the other. For some people, this much space would be a studio apartment. Here, it was a cozy enclave.

"Hang tight. I'll get the cobbler and coffee."

Miles darted back into the house before I could say anything. I looked out and up to the star-filled night sky. It was even quieter here than at the inn. I guessed because the house was tucked away from the main part of town. In the summer, it'd be stunning, spending an evening here as night enveloped the island.

Clattering behind me signaled Miles was trying to open the door. I hurried over to assist.

"Thanks," he said as I took the book he had jammed under his arm so he could better maneuver with the tray. "Coffee, cobbler, and photos."

"Perfect." I took a seat next to Miles on the couch and served the chocolatey dessert while he poured the beverage.

I moaned as I inhaled the bowl of molten chocolate goo. I couldn't get a bite in fast enough. Is this what living with Miles would be like? Stunning landscapes, delicious food, curled up on a couch with him in the evenings? Chicago had nothing on this.

"That's the best thing I've ever tasted." I followed up immediately with another bite.

"Right? It's crazy good. The chewy brownie, the liquid chocolate. I'd be happy to drown in a dish of it."

He set down his bowl, wiped his hands on one of the napkins he'd brought, and opened the book between us. The first page featured a black-and-white picture of the Grand Hotel with film equipment surrounding the porch.

"The pictures I promised," he said. He flipped pages slowly as he told stories. "Dad was on the transportation crew helping haul stuff around the island with our carriages, so he was usually at the major filming locations. He had a Brownie camera, and he took tons of pictures. It was a pretty old-school way to take pictures even in seventy-nine, but he loved it. He actually developed these in the workshop."

"These are fantastic. They should be on the DVD extras."

"When they were doing the most recent version, they asked if he'd license some, but he declined. It was one thing to show them at the Grand for the convention goers, but he didn't want to outright sell them."

He talked through page after page of pictures from the various places I'd seen on the location tour. We took turns with who ate and who turned the pages, careful to keep the book clean. The candids with the stars as they were setting up scenes were my favorites. The last page of the book was the best of all—Christopher Reeve squatting to the same level as a young Miles, dressed in his Superman T-shirt.

"That's amazing." I skimmed my hand just over the surface of the photo. It was easy to see the man sitting next to me in the child from the photo. He was adorable, looking at Reeve with awe. "You look like you're actually meeting Superman."

"I thought I was, or meeting Clark Kent, anyway. My dad says I asked him where his glasses were."

I laughed. "Oh my God. That's way too cute."

Miles took the book and set it on the coffee table, next to our empty dessert dishes. He snuggled in next to me, arm across the back of the couch but close enough it brushed against my neck. Despite only knowing Miles less than a week, I felt like I belonged here. It didn't make sense, but I wasn't going to question it.

I scooched over and nestled in as his hand dropped to cover my shoulder. I was pretty sure I could stay here, forever.

"You cold?" Miles asked, voice barely above a whisper.

"Nope."

Miles kissed the side of my head with the softest peck, and I let go of a long sigh.

"I haven't felt like this in a long time," I said without moving.

"How so?"

"This... comfortable." I adjusted so I was still snuggled close but angled my head so I could see him better. "You make me feel like I'm supposed to be here."

We held each other's gazes for a moment before he spoke. "Maybe you are." He ran his free hand over his beard. "We'll just have to see where it goes."

"I've been thinking about that. I can come up here often."

"I'll come to see you too, especially in the winter when business is slow and the staff can handle everything."

"Caleb will like that," I said as Miles raised an eyebrow. "You can't tell me Caleb isn't grooming himself to take over the business with all the work he's doing."

A happy laugh spilled from Miles. "He's definitely got a future with horses if he wants it, whether it's with me or a place of his own." He shifted the conversation back to the original topic. "Do you think it's foolish to try this long distance?"

"If there's one thing I've learned from the movie, you have to take certain chances when it comes to finding the love of your life. I need to know if that's you."

"I knew from your bumbling words when I took you to get the fudge that I felt something with you."

Heat warmed my face as Miles hit the embarrassment button.

I brought his head to mine so I could kiss him. The kisses were tender. Getting to know Miles on a more intimate level was intoxicating. It was a good thing we were sitting because I wasn't sure if I could stand.

Time had no meaning while we were making out. In the moments I stole glances at him, he looked blissful, and if I caught him with his eyes open, they were alive with passion.

When he pulled back just enough so I couldn't reach his lips, it felt like a lifeline had been pulled away.

"I hope I'm not too forward by asking this, but would you like to go upstairs?"

I'd never seen him look so shy, or sexy.

I nodded as I stood and offered him a hand. He kept my hand in his as we went back through the kitchen to the stairs at the front of the house.

"We'll save the tour for later." His tone was playful as he led me into one of the bedrooms and flicked the light switch.

The room fit him perfectly with its warm earth tones. It had a modern edge with the furnishings streamlined and less antique than what was downstairs.

"This isn't romantic lighting at all. One second." He zipped across the room and turned on a lamp behind a cozy-looking leather chair that appeared to be part of a reading nook. He returned and extinguished the overhead light. "That's better."

My heart was about to pop out of my chest since my anticipation level was off the charts. I was drunk, but not because of alcohol—it was this man, who was gorgeous, powerful, and yet so gentle.

"I don't know what I want to do." Shyness crept into Miles's voice. "I don't wanna mess us up."

"I'm glad you're nervous too," I whispered. Again, we looked at each other, and he made me feel like the most special person on Earth. "I know what I want to do, though."

His response was the smallest nod. I grabbed the hem of his shirt, lifted it slowly, revealing a flat stomach with a dark blond treasure trail disappearing into his jeans. He raised his hands so there was no trouble getting the shirt off, but I took my time. Once I got past his stomach, fine blond hairs, similar to the dusting on his arms, led the way up to his chest. The higher I went, the more there was and the darker it became to match what I'd seen around his belly button. His nipples were taunt, either from the chill outside or his arousal. I grazed one as I continued lifting the shirt. He gasped, and I grinned at discovering the sensitivity.

Once it was off, I unceremoniously dropped it to the floor. I'd wondered for days what he looked like shirtless, and I wasn't disappointed. Hard work had honed his body—just like I thought it would be—into a powerfully built chest and arms. I ran my hands over the exposed skin, making sure to gently brush each nipple. A small sigh escaped both of us.

"My turn." His grin was impish. "This sweater looks great, but it's time for it to go."

He wasn't slow in getting the sweater off. My body wasn't like his, but I was fit enough. He seemed to like what he saw as he drew me in and wrapped his arms around me. When he started running his hands across my back in a sort of massage, I was putty in his hands, and my moans made that clear.

The bulge in his jeans made itself known, and feeling it against mine made it difficult not to grind into him. I pulled back just enough to give us space to kiss. It wasn't gentle this time. Pressed against his bare chest, a fire lit that I wasn't going to ignore. He clearly felt the same way as we went at it with an intensity that made our previous make-out session in the office seem G-rated. Every time I slipped my hand between us and tweaked one of his nipples, he shuddered. I loved that.

"Can we please get out of these?" He pulled on the waist of my jeans.

He was working the button of his jeans before I could respond. It was a race to see who could become pants-less first. He ended up in a pair of red briefs, and I could see why I'd felt him through the jeans as the fabric strained to contain him. My boxers were far looser, but my tent was also quite pronounced.

"Don't stop there," he said before dropping his briefs.

"Nah, I'm good just looking at you." I put my hands on my hips. "You're one big boy, kinda all over."

It was hard to tell in the low light, but I swear the slightest bit of blush crept across his cheeks. I licked my lips, trying to hold my ground rather than just pouncing on him.

He raised a questioning eyebrow before coming deliberately toward me. It felt like it took him forever to close the space, and that only raised the heat factor.

"Please?" He slipped a finger under the waistband and moved it along my skin. He didn't pull them down, but he teased me just right.

"How can I say no to that?"

This time, he raised both eyebrows before he lowered his gaze and pushed the shorts down with both hands.

The smallest grunt escaped his lips before he spoke. "So perfect."

He grabbed my hand, led us to the bed, and pulled me on top of him. I positioned myself so one of my legs was between his, which aligned our bodies just right.

I didn't make it back to the inn because neither one of us felt like leaving after getting to know each other very well. It was all we could do to clean up just enough so we wouldn't wake up in a sticky mess.

SIXTEEN

"Hey, Miles, this is a pleasant surprise," I said as I answered my cell phone. I did my best to sound awake even though the alarm had only gone off a couple of minutes earlier.

After a stunning few days with Miles before I'd returned to Chicago, we were talking multiple times a day. I missed him terribly, but the phone calls were getting me through. This was an odd call because it was ridiculously early in the morning.

"Didn't wake you, did I?" he asked.

"Nope, but I haven't gotten out of bed yet either."

"Perfect," he sorta growled. "Me either." My phone dinged with a text message. "See?"

"Oooh. Let me look."

I flipped over to the message and found a picture of Miles, covers just above his waist showing his beautiful stomach and chest. He wore only a sleepy smile. I'd seen that look in person several mornings, because after we slept together the first time, I was in his bed every night. My room at the inn had become only the place I worked during the day.

"Oh, man." I brought the phone back to my ear. "Wish I was waking up to that sexiness in person."

"Me too." He spoke sleepily, lazily. "Show me you."

"You're bad this morning." I put him on speaker so I could maneuver the phone and take a picture like his. "What's gotten into you?"

"Like you have to ask. It didn't take long for me to get addicted to you."

"Coming back at you." I sent the photo.

It was weird sending it. The one time I sent Drake a shirtless pic, he told me not to do that because someone might steal it and post it somewhere. I didn't get the big deal since you couldn't see any more than if I was at a beach. Getting the sexy surprise from Miles was awesome and something I wanted to encourage.

"So I know you haven't even been gone a week, but I was thinking I'd come down this weekend. If it's okay with you."

"Hell yes!"

"That was even more enthusiastic than I was hoping for." His happiness radiated out from the speaker.

I got rid of the blanket so the tent my cock made against the sheet showed clearly. I snapped a pic and sent it.

"How's that for enthusiastic?"

"That's not fair," he said through a moan, "showing me what I can't have."

"It's all yours this weekend."

"Hmmmmm.... Mine's happy to hear that."

As if the initial moan wasn't enough, he groaned on, making my cock pulse under the sheets. The phone chirped again.

"Fuck me." It was barely a whisper, and I couldn't be sure Miles even heard it. I made sure to speak louder. "Talk about no fair."

The picture was him, holding his erection with a drop of precum right at the tip. I grabbed my dick. If he was going to play like that, so was I. I clicked off another picture with my free hand.

"Oh yeah," Miles said shortly after I heard the ping of the image arriving on his phone.

"You gonna save that for me?" It wasn't a fair question since I was gently pulling on my cock, knowing I wasn't going to be able to save mine.

"What do I get if I save it? It's a long time until Friday."

The idea of him saving a load was appealing. What could he build up if he gave it some time? I squeezed my shaft to release more precum so I had some lube to work with. I was suddenly a horny teenager again, getting off to pics of hot men.

"You seemed to like it when I sat on that massive tool. What if I do that again?"

The low, long growl meant I'd struck a nerve. "You were so tight. I'd have a hard time not blowing before you got all the way down."

"I bet." I paused to make him wonder what I might say next. "I can make you hold on until I'm ready for you to blow."

Miles was breathing harder. I'd gotten to him just like I wanted. The first time he was inside me, he lost himself quickly. I hadn't minded because the pleasure running through both of us triggered me to come at practically the same time. I'd never taken someone as big as him, and it'd been a long time since he topped, so it was nearly impossible to make it last. I knew how to control a top, though, and the next time he wouldn't unload so fast.

"You're jerking it right now," I said.

"Am not."

"Are too. And I hear you struggling not to let on."

We ended up giggling. I was so carefree with Miles, unlike any of my other boyfriends. Something about him made it so I could just be however I wanted to be in the moment. It was refreshing.

"Should I be embarrassed that I can't hide things from you even when you're hundreds of miles away?"

"Of course not. It's not like I'm not lying here ever so slowly working mine."

"Saying things like that doesn't help me stop."

"Oh, I know." I hit a sensitive spot just under my cockhead that had me extending out the end of the word by several syllables.

"Fuck, Jordan. What did you just do?" God, his voice got so low and sexy sometimes. "There's no way I'm going to be—" He lost himself in a moan, and then there was the clatter of the phone falling.

"You okay?"

"Damn it." The voice came from a distance. "Oh fuck." There were several intense grunts too.

My cock was all too aware of the sounds he made.

"Jordan?" He sounded out of breath.

"Yeah. What just happened?"

"I dropped the phone and it slid off the bed." He held back a laugh. "I rolled over, and as I got to the side of the bed, I came while sliding my dick across the sheets. It's a helluva mess here."

That's all my cock needed to know. Even though I wasn't stroking intensely, the magic line was crossed, and there was no stopping me. I tightened my grip, and it took just a few strokes to shoot ropes of jizz across my chest as I moaned into the phone.

"Yes!" Miles sounded as if he'd just won a game. "Love that sound."

"Talk about a mess." I angled the phone and snapped a pic of the aftermath. "Even though you didn't save it. I'm still going to ride you until you beg to come."

"What if I pound the cum out of *you* instead." His sound got muffled again. "You weren't kidding about that mess."

"We'll see exactly who controls the situation. Gonna be freakin' hot either way."

"Indeed."

"Show me your cum."

In just a few seconds, I had the picture. It was hard to make out what was on the white sheets, but there were some wet spots. Most impressive was the cum that was matted into the hair on his abs.

"If I was there, I'd be cleaning you up."

"Mmmmm. I could save that for you?"

"Um, no. Fresh cum only please."

More soft laughter. "It's good to know where your limits are. So I should get up and get a move on."

"Yeah, same here. Talk to you later today?"

"For sure. Later, Jordan."

"Bye."

I clicked off and dropped the phone on the bed next to me. What an amazing way to wake up. It would've been better if he'd actually been in my bed, but it was still scorching hot. The week was destined to go at a snail's pace while I waited for him to arrive.

SEVENTEEN

"He's fun," Alberto said after Miles excused himself and went to the restroom. We'd just finished dinner and were contemplating dessert. "I've never seen you so happy and comfortable. I've known every boyfriend you've ever had, and this one.... Well...." I raised an eyebrow at Alberto. Did he see something I didn't? Why was he hesitating? "It kinda makes me believe in the idea of a soul mate."

I couldn't stop my biggest grin ever.

"I want someone to look at me like you two look at each other," he continued. "I'm really happy for you. So what are you guys going to get up to while he's here?"

The abrupt shift in conversation made sense as Miles returned and sat next to me. He looked awesome tonight. Casual but dressy as we came to Spiaggia for the best Italian in the city. It was one of my favorites, and Alberto nailed it by snagging the reservation for the three of us.

"Okay, so I'm sure you two were talking about me while I was gone. Did I pass the best friend test?" I opened my mouth, and he raised his hand before I could say anything. "Just remember, Luke thinks you're great."

"You pass every test," Alberto said. "You're the best guy he's ever introduced me to."

"Hear that?" Miles puffed his chest out. "Best ever."

"I don't need to be convinced." I leaned over to kiss his cheek, trying not to get caught up in the scratchy feel of his beard.

"Now, now, no need to make out at the table," Alberto said. "Plenty of time for that later."

"Jordan, Alberto, what a nice surprise." I turned to find Roy Bell coming toward the table. Roy was one of our regular investors for the projects we managed.

"Roy, great to see you." I stood to shake his hand. "I was glad to see we've got a meeting next week."

"Roy." Alberto stood to greet him as well. "A pleasure as always."

"Yes," he said, "my team's got some new strategies we want to discuss. You'll get details Monday so we can have a productive meeting."

"Excellent," I said. "Roy, this is my boyfriend, Miles Colter."

Miles stood. "Pleasure to meet you."

"Good to meet you as well," Roy said as he shook Miles's hand.

Alberto gave me a quick worried look before he turned back to Roy to discuss next week. I saw what concerned him right after. Drake had walked in and was coming toward us. His face clouded over as he looked past Roy and saw me. Hopefully, his need to present the best front would hold true since Roy was a joint client.

"Roy, great to see you're already here," Drake said, interrupting Alberto as he clapped Roy on the shoulder. "Alberto, Jordan, good to see you both. Miles, I trust things are easier now that everything's settled with the family stables since this one"—he gestured with his head to me—"swooped in like an angel to invest such a hefty sum."

No one knew about that except Alberto and our firm's financial officer. How'd Drake get that information? It took all my self-control not to climb over the table and throttle Drake. But, I had to keep up a facade for Roy, and Drake knew that.

"It's good to be back on solid ground," Miles said without missing a beat. I was probably the only one who noticed the coldness that seeped into his eyes.

Fuck. Fuck. Fuck. Drake loved to stir things up.

"We should sit." Drake moved past Roy, indicating for the hostess to move on.

"Good to see you both, and nice to meet you, Miles." Roy either didn't realize what had happened or had the good grace not to acknowledge it.

"What'd Drake mean by that?" Miles's stare was awful. I wanted to crawl under the table and curl into a ball. "You said it was spread among investors, but he made it sound like it's all you."

My mind raced, but it was scrambled by the fear of losing Miles and seething anger for what Drake had done.

"The way our deals are structured," Alberto started, but I held up my hand so he'd stop. This was my mess and mine to clean up.

"There are two investors in the stables. One is our company and the other is me."

"What?" Despite the fact he kept his voice low, his fury was crystal clear.

"Remember I'd told you I wasn't sure if our regular investors would sign on for something so far outside our normal offerings? It was true. So we structured the deal this way."

"You didn't think you should tell me that? Jesus, Jordan, that's a lot of money."

"It's fine. I invest all the time."

"It's not *fine,* and the fact you can't see that makes it all the worse." He stood before I could grab for his arm. "I need to go."

The guy lived on an island with few people, but he knew how to behave in crowds. No doubt that was honed by years of not wanting to make a scene that would spread around town. He calmly walked out. Drake managed to orchestrate the quietest public outburst I'd ever seen. Fucking bastard.

"How'd he find out?" Alberto looked like he'd been punched in the gut.

"I have no idea," I said. "It doesn't seem—"

"Oh no." Alberto's face fell. "Drake was in the office for a meeting on Friday. I caught him in your office afterward. He said he was dropping something off. He must've seen something. Dammit. I shouldn't have taken him on his word."

"I don't remember seeing anything from him. But the folder with the investment paperwork was on the desk." I stood hastily, bumping the table and knocking over what was left of a glass of wine. "I gotta go."

Alberto nodded. "I'll take care of the check. Go get him."

"Thanks."

Following Miles's example, I walked out as if nothing was wrong. Miles had come with me, so he was either on foot or in a cab. "Did you see where the blond guy went when he left?" I asked the valet.

"He's just down the block." He gestured with a jerk of his head.

I turned and found Miles standing at a storefront—one hand on the glass while the other held his phone. He was slightly hunched over like he might be sick.

"Hey," I said when I got to him, "you okay?"

He stood straight, wiped at his eyes, and spun around.

"Not even close." His voice was tightly controlled. "You lied to me. Why would you do that?"

"I didn't tell you because I didn't want this."

"We wouldn't have had this fight because I wouldn't have let you do it in the first place." He closed the space between us, and I fought the urge to flinch because he looked like he might throw a punch. "You knew I wasn't asking people for help. Random investors was one thing, but you? The man I'm falling so hard for, putting up all that cash."

"Miles, it was the only way. You were on your way to losing everything. I was going to put up some money no matter what because I'm your friend."

"And you thought going behind my back was a good idea? What does that mean for us down the road? What else would you keep to yourself?"

"Miles—"

"I can't." He stole a glance at this phone and stepped to the curb as a car drove up—Uber sticker in the corner. "I can't do this."

"Wait."

He slammed the door, nearly taking my hand with him. The car pulled away before I could do anything.

He had to go back to my place. His luggage was there, and since he had a key, I had to hurry before he could get away. The wait for my car was excruciating. A party of five, who, of course, all drove separate cars, was ahead of me. The five minutes it took to get my car seemed like forever.

More than enough time for Miles to get his stuff and disappear.

I'd really fucked this up. He said he was falling hard for me. We were on the precipice of something huge, and this was going to wreck it all.

Driving, I seemed to hit every red light in the city. I texted Miles and pleaded with him to stay until I got home. There was no response.

And Drake, I knew he had an angry streak, but I had no idea he'd do something so vengeful.

I pulled up in the circle of my building and tossed the keys to the valet. In the elevator, too many people stopping on lower floors impeded my progress to twenty-five. Thankfully, I didn't fumble my keys at the lock. I felt like I was going to fly apart at the seams by the time I got inside. I was terrified at what I'd done, and I couldn't stop shaking as a result.

Nothing looked different as I entered. In the bedroom, his discarded clothes were still on the floor where I'd stripped him so he could dress for dinner. His small bag was on the floor next to the dresser.

Somehow, I'd beaten him here. Hopefully, I'd be able make him understand that I'd just wanted to help. I didn't want to blow what was turning into the best thing that'd ever happened to me. Alberto had said it at dinner—Miles made me crazy happy. He wasn't the only one who was falling hard.

I dropped onto the couch to wait. He had to be here soon, unless he was just having the driver take him around the city. I'd wait, we'd talk, and it'd be fine.

It had to be.

EIGHTEEN

Miles didn't come back. He went home, leaving the few things he'd brought at my apartment. He finally answered a text Saturday night, saying he'd gone home. Before I could ask, he said he didn't care what I did with his luggage.

What was supposed to be an awesome weekend had gone to hell. I knew exactly how Richard Collier felt when he was yanked back to 1980 because of the stray penny in his pocket. I'd been living in a fantasy world that was pulled out from under me. It'd been hard enough to come back to Chicago when all I wanted to do with stay with Miles on the island. Now, everything was in shambles.

I gently packed up his clothes and toiletries. I couldn't throw them out, so I figured I'd ship it back at some point.

After two days spent mostly staring at the ceiling, I had to get back to work. There were meetings I couldn't blow off. Luckily, I knew how to flip a switch inside my brain to be *on* for business so I don't think anyone knew how out of sorts I was.

"Damn, man, I've seen you do presentations with the

flu, but I've never seen a performance like you just gave," Alberto said, coming back to the conference room after showing our prospective client out. "You did a great job. I think that deal's going to close."

I slumped in the chair I'd been in for the past three hours.

"What can I do?" he asked.

"I don't think there's anything. He's cut me off." I looked at Alberto as he sat in a chair across the table from me. "Thank you for not saying *I told you so* or something like that."

"You know I'd never do that to you."

"True. In the future, though, be more emphatic about not letting me do stupid shit like this."

He simply nodded, and I laid my head on the cool wood of the conference table. Sleep had come in fits and starts since Friday, and I was exhausted. Rest eluded me as I kept thinking about what I'd done.

"If you start to turn gray, I'm calling the paramedics." He was trying to lighten the mood, but there was no laughter in me.

"It hurts so much." My voice was muffled since my face was against the table.

Saying that broke the dam of my emotions. Outbursts aren't usually my thing, but I couldn't hold back any longer.

"Whoa, Jordan." Alberto was quickly by my side, wrapping an arm around my shoulders as I sat up. "You'll get through this, and not alone."

"Through it, sure," I managed to say between gasps and sobs. "But not with him."

"You don't know that. It's only been three days. He'll think it through and see that he overreacted."

"He looked so hurt and angry."

There was a knock at the door.

"Hang on." Alberto squeezed my shoulder before he went to the door.

I dropped my head back to the table, hoping not to be seen.

"Yes?" he said, opening the door.

"There's a Luke on the phone for Jordan," Madison, our receptionist, said. "Says he's a friend and it's urgent that he talks to him."

"Take a message, please—"

"No." I willed myself to stop being a mess. "I'll take it."

Alberto still blocked the door, but Madison said, "He's on line three. Alberto, can you return Drake's call? He's been calling practically every five minutes because you haven't been returning calls or emails. I've told him—"

"Let's take this outside." Alberto turned back to me. "We'll give you some privacy." He slipped out the door.

I steeled myself. This wasn't going to be a good phone call. How did Luke even track me down? Was Miles making him deliver a message? I had to pick up the phone to find out but was scared this was the final nail in our relationship coffin. One last deep breath and I answered.

"Hello?"

"Jordan?"

At least he didn't seem angry.

"Yeah."

"You don't sound like yourself. I guess I shouldn't be surprised. Miles isn't right either. What the heck happened? He was gaga when he left Friday morning. Turns out he got back Saturday morning, went straight to his place, and didn't surface until I rousted him this morning. All he'd say is that you guys were done. He went to work like a zombie."

I sighed. I'd destroyed both of us.

"Jordan?" he finally asked after I'd let too much silence slip by.

"I'm here."

"I know it may not be any of my business, but my best friend's hurting and won't talk. I know we don't know each other well, but you were good for Miles—"

"I kept a secret I shouldn't have," I blurted out. Luke got the abbreviated story of how I managed to save Colter Stables but wrecked the relationship with its owner.

"That explains a lot. He's one of the proudest, most protective people I know. Always has been. Especially where family stuff's concerned. He gets it from his dad, who was always quick to offer help to anyone but never wanted it to look like he might need some."

I itched to get up and move around. It was rare for me to take a call without pacing, but I couldn't do that with this phone.

"When we were ten," Luke continued, "Miles's parents and Nate all came down with some nasty flu. When he hadn't shown up for school for a couple of days, I went around to see what was up. He tried to swear me to secrecy that he was taking care of them and it'd be fine in a few days. I couldn't keep that secret, and boy was he pissed at me when I turned up later with my mom. It took him weeks to speak to me again."

"I've really fucked up, haven't I?"

"I won't sugarcoat it. I haven't seen him this upset since Nate bailed. He's managed other breakups better than what I've seen this morning. I'd called ready to give it to you for breaking his heart. I could tell by the way you answered, though, that more was going on."

We were quiet, so quiet that I thought he might've hung

up. I didn't know what to say. Luke's story simply drove home how much I'd mismanaged the situation.

"He's been so happy with you." Luke filled the silence. "You brought him out like I haven't seen in a long while. And even though I know him well, I don't know what to tell you about how to fix this."

"I'm coming up there," I said suddenly. "It'll be hard to run away from each other if we're both on the island. I'd been thinking about it anyway. There's nothing to lose because it can't get any worse. I'll try to get there today."

"If there's anything I can do, let me know. I'm willing to have him pissed at me if there's a chance to get you guys talking."

"Thanks. I owe you a beer while I'm there."

"See you soon," he said before he hung up.

I dropped the phone back in its cradle. This was the only option—a face-to-face. Richard didn't give up until he proved himself to Elise. I had to prove myself to Miles.

Alberto knocked before coming in.

"I saw the line disconnect. What's going on?"

"It was Miles's best friend. Miles isn't doing great either. I'm gonna go up there." I stood and came around to Alberto. "I'm sorry, but can you manage without me for the rest of the week?"

"Of course. You're not going to be much good moping around anyway. You need to get up there and try to patch things up."

I clapped him on the shoulder and went to my office. He followed close behind. "What was all that about Drake?"

"Nothing for you to worry about."

I stopped short of my desk and faced Alberto and

cocked my eyebrow. We had a brief, silent standoff before he relented.

"I've no doubt he's pissed at me." I leaned against my desk, making it clear I wasn't going anywhere until he spilled. He sighed and continued. "While I was paying the check, he stepped outside to take a call and Roy came over to talk. He was concerned he'd said something wrong because of the tension at the table."

"I hope you assured him that he did nothing."

"Oh, I did. I told him it was Drake saying some things he shouldn't have."

"You're evil." I couldn't help but grin at what he'd done, even though it could be devastating for Drake since clients expect discretion.

"Drake's the evil one. Anyway, Roy emailed last night asking if we could recommend someone as he no longer feels comfortable working with Drake."

"No wonder Drake wants to talk to you."

"I'll deal with it. And he totally deserves it." He pulled on my arm to get me off the desk. "You need to get going."

"I'll be back as soon as I can. And, I guess, sooner rather than later if I strike out."

"Don't strike out."

I pulled Alberto into a hug. "I won't."

I grabbed my bag and stuffed my laptop into it. In the lobby, I stopped at Madison's desk.

"Can you please call one of the private jet services and book a flight to Mackinac Island as soon as possible? I want to land on the island. It'll be a one-way trip. I'll worry about getting back later."

"Of course. Any cost ceiling?"

"Not this time. Just put it on my personal card."

She smiled, nodded, and turned to her keyboard. "I'll send you the details as soon as it's done."

I bolted home to pack. By the time I finished, Madison had let me know a pilot would be waiting at Executive Field.

NINETEEN

The flight was only a few hours, but by the time we touched down at the island's small airfield, I still had no plan. I strategize all the time, but in this case, I didn't know what the right move was. It was a wonder I could think at all since I had the shakes like I'd had a zillion cups of coffee. It was make or break time.

As I stepped off the plane, the chilly air hit me and reminded me of him—particularly of the night we watched the sunset. I don't know why. It was midafternoon and we weren't near the shoreline, but something about the breeze carried him.

Walking into the small terminal, I realized I hadn't done anything about transportation. Since I was on a private charter, it wasn't like there'd be anyone waiting. I saw the sign for Colter Stables along with other signs offering rides from the airport. My heart ached. I couldn't call my preferred carriage company. I didn't have a plan, but Miles picking up the phone was not the right choice.

The walk into downtown wouldn't be too bad. I only had my messenger bag and an overnight bag, so a walk would have to do. I didn't need word of my arrival spreading around any faster than necessary. Plans changed, however, when I walked outside and found Caleb waiting with a carriage.

"Jordan?" he said, surprised.

"Caleb. What brought you up here?"

"Saw the plane, and since I'd finished a delivery, I thought I'd swing up to see if anyone needed a ride. Does Miles know you're here?"

I shook my head.

"Sorry. My momma would knock me in the head for butting in. I just know he's moping."

"I hope to fix that."

"Good." Caleb spoke quietly, as if uncomfortable broaching the topic. "Do you want to go see him? He's probably still at the stable."

I tossed the bags into the carriage and climbed in.

"Not yet. Can you take me to the inn so I can get a room? Gotta make sure I have a place to crash if this goes wrong."

"Sure."

We rode silently into town. Thankfully, as we arrived at the inn, an idea finally struck.

"Can you wait while I take this inside and then drop me off somewhere else?" I asked as I stepped out.

"Of course."

I ran inside like a man possessed. In fact, Mrs. Tanner looked at me like I'd gone mad, especially since I'd shown up out of the blue. She gave me my old room, and let me store my bags in the parlor until I returned.

Back in the carriage, I asked Caleb to take me to the tree where Richard and Elise first met. Miles had taken us there on the tour during the convention. If there was romantic power anywhere on the island, it *had* to be there. Excitement crept in, replacing some of the chaos that had swirled in my brain all morning.

"Do you think you can get him to come see me?" I felt bad asking Caleb to take part in the plan, but it seemed the most direct thing.

"I'll come up with something to send him this way. If I can't, I bet Luke'll help."

"You've talked to Luke?"

"He thought he saw you go into the inn. He texted me to find out."

"Small-town news chain in progress."

"Oh yeah, nothing escapes it."

"How do you live with that? I'd have gone insane at your age if I knew people were always watching."

"You learn tricks." He sounded very much like the teenager he was.

"Shouldn't you be in school anyway?"

"Only had morning classes. So today I go to school, work a while, and then homework. Benefits of being a senior."

As we traveled on the road along the shore, all I could think about was the night we watched the sunset from the spot farther north. It was a perfect moment, like all the moments with Miles. I still didn't know what I was going to say to him—other than sorry a few hundred times.

My heart pounded so loudly, by the time we arrived at the tree, I expected Caleb to make a comment about it.

"Thanks, Caleb. For everything."

"You're welcome." Before he got the carriage underway, he turned back. "Good luck."

I nodded as he headed north. As the clip-clop faded away, I looked at the plaque that was set into the large bolder marking this spot. Running my hands over the plaque's lettering for the movie's title and the "Is it you?" quote, I tried to draw inspiration for what I'd say when Miles got there.

Those simple words started it for Richard and Elise. What was I going to say to get Miles and me back on track? How did I say I'm sorry for keeping his family's business safe? Actually, that's not what I had to apologize for—it was for hiding how I was doing it.

I circled behind the boulder and leaned against it. It didn't take long for the cold to seep through my jeans. It'd be amazing to wait for Miles here for a guaranteed happy reunion, like if I'd been away and was coming home early as a surprise.

The now-familiar sound of a horse on the road approached. It was only one, and I didn't hear carriage wheels. Could it be? It didn't seem like enough time had passed. Looking toward the road, I found Miles and Wildfire approaching. Terror vibrated through me. This was my one chance to make amends.

"It's pretty ballsy of you to come up here." Miles came to a stop just on the other side of the boulder I rested against.

"I had to." I pushed off the rock and calmly moved toward Wildfire. I wasn't sure who I was trying to spook less—the horse or its rider. "We can't leave things like they are. Even if it means we're through. All I wanted to do was help."

"How could you not tell me? Not give me the chance to say no, or to maybe say yes. It was a huge leap for me to say yes to the investment offer, especially after all the trouble the last loan caused. But to find out you're the one who put up the majority of cash?"

I reached out to Wildfire and scratched his neck. He nuzzled his head against my hand as I stroked. At least he still liked me.

"I'm not a millionaire, but I've got savings and I maintain investments. Colter Stables is an investment I believe in —both in the business and its owner. Yes, I'm helping you. But it'll also pay a fair profit during the expected span of the deal."

"Do you know how much it hurt to have it talked about like that? And from Drake no less?"

"I think I have a pretty good idea."

I wanted to reach out to him, even if it was just to squeeze his leg.

"Why did you even tell him?"

"I didn't." He raised an eyebrow but didn't interrupt. "He was in our offices last week. Alberto caught him in my office, and we think he found the paperwork on my desk."

He didn't speak, but he finally dismounted Wildfire so we were on even ground.

"Hurting you was the last thing I wanted." I took his hands in mine. "I love you. There it is. I've said it. You need to know that's how I feel." My chest clenched, and I fought back tears as my voice cracked. "You make me happy, more than I've been in years. I want to keep seeing you. We need to find out everything about each other—the good and bad. Do we get to have that chance?"

He looked conflicted, but nowhere near how he was on the street before he'd left Chicago.

"I've often been told I'm too proud and stubborn for my own good. While that may be true, you have to understand that I work hard and don't want charity."

"This isn't—"

"I let you talk. It's my turn." His voice was measured, as

if he was trying to keep his emotions at bay. "I know this isn't charity. It's a business deal. But you sold me on it because it sounded like several investors were going to take part in keeping the stables going. Instead I find out it's you and your business. Don't get me wrong, I'm thankful my family legacy is safe. But it's one man—someone I was building a relationship with—responsible for that. How do I move forward with someone I'm also indebted to? I'm falling in love with you too. But I'm so torn."

His hands flexed in my grip. It was a slight movement, and I wasn't sure what it meant. Did he even know he was doing it?

"If we keep going," I suggested, "maybe we end up family, and then it'd be family helping family."

"That's making a pretty big leap, don't you think?"

The slightest hint of a smile played on his lips, and I was elated to see it. I reached out to touch the corner of his mouth.

"I've missed that." I dropped my hand back to my side. "Look, this all turned out wrong. The investment was a way to make sure your business was safe, that was all. I'm not taking the support back if you send me away. But you should know that my heart's yours if you still want it."

I quaked, my emotions on the verge of spilling out like they had in the conference room.

Without warning, he pulled me toward him, took his hands from mine, and wrapped his arms around me. I'm not sure who was shaking more, him or me. I hugged him hard.

"I'll take yours if you'll take mine." He buried his face against my neck.

I simply nodded. Wildfire nudged us, as if giving his approval. Miles let go after a few moments.

"Come on, we've got some serious making up to do.

Wildfire," he said, stroking the side of the horse, "think you can manage us both for a little bit?" He gave the horse a final pat. "You get on first, then slide in behind the saddle. You'll hang on to this." He patted the back of the saddle. "Not to me. Not crazy comfortable, but we won't be traveling far."

Once we were both on Wildfire and the horse seemed none the worse for wear, Miles got us underway.

TWENTY

Miles tied Wildfire to the front porch, and we scrambled to get into the house before we pulled off each other's clothes.

"Hang on, one second," Miles said, already sounding breathless.

He pulled his phone from his jeans and started typing.

"Texting, really?" I said with mock annoyance.

"Gotta have Caleb come get Wildfire. Wouldn't be good for him to stay out overnight, and I suspect we're not leaving the house until morning."

"You're right about that."

I pulled off my boots and jacket and parked them in the hallway where they belonged. Then I removed my sweatshirt and threw it at Miles's head as he typed.

"I'll be upstairs when you're finally done with that."

Before I got too far, I tossed my T-shirt at him too.

"Hey, wait for me." I'd already entered the bedroom, but the clomping of his boots indicated he was coming up the stairs fast—two-at-a-time from the sound of it.

He found me dropping my jeans as he entered and began fumbling with his own clothes.

"Wildfire taken care of?" I tossed my briefs in his direction.

"Yeah."

His breath caught as he watched me lie back on the bed with my cock at attention.

"I've been waiting to get you naked since those texts last week," I said.

He was less than graceful getting out of his clothes, and I had to contain my laughter. Once he was naked, he stood at the foot of the bed, fixing me with a smoldering look that made me squirm in delight. He didn't make a move to join me, though. He just watched. I gave him a bit of a show—lightly caressing my hardness, making it pulse, running a finger across my balls. He licked his lips, but still didn't come for me.

Squeezing my cock released a drop of precum. I smiled at him as I licked it off my finger. Repeating the action, I got more and then crawled to him, making sure not to lose the tasty treat on the tip of my finger.

Once I was in front of him, his cock was at mouth level, so I licked just the head, where I got a yummy taste of my own. Kneeling before him, I put my finger against his lips, and he licked the liquid off, seductively moving his tongue around. When he was finished, he took my hand.

"Have I told you how incredible you look?" He grabbed my dick with his free hand. "The whole package is kinda perfect, in and out of clothes."

Suddenly, he crashed his mouth against mine. The aggressiveness of the kisses overtook me. It was like we were both afraid this wouldn't last. My body hummed from the urgency. I couldn't get enough.

I tugged on his shoulders to get him to join me on the bed. We moaned as our bodies collapsed together, slightly rougher than I'd intended but majorly hot. The pleasure flowing through me was intense and threatened to make me come before we'd even begun.

It was tough, but I forced myself to focus on just the kissing and not the sensations everywhere else. I needed to last because I wanted to give him the ride I'd promised him. It was time for me to take over. I rolled us so Miles was on his back.

I scrambled across the bed to get to the condoms and lube. "Seems like I owe you a little something."

"Oh, man. I haven't come in days. Not since we were on the phone the other day. I was saving it for the trip, and then when I got back...."

I put three fingers on his lips. "That doesn't matter now. We're here, together, and it's all good. Just lie back."

The condom packet easily ripped open, and I rolled the sheath over his throbbing cock, which was already lubed up with precum. Miles adjusted the pillows beneath his head.

"Comfy?" I asked as I lubed us up.

"Yeah. And I'm gonna have a good view."

Swinging a leg over him, I positioned myself over his cock. He couldn't have it that easy, though, so I slid his head along my crack instead of letting it in. Miles shuddered between my thighs while the teasing continued.

"You're evil."

"Maybe a little." I reached behind to spread my cheeks wide. "Try this."

Sitting back, I aligned his cock at the entrance to my ass. We moaned in sync again. Miles was so eager, but he kept himself in check, knowing I was in charge this time.

Reaching around again, I grabbed his shaft to steady it

while I sat. He was large, and his head pressed against my hole. A few deep breaths helped me relax against the pressure he was applying. The head suddenly slipped inside, and he reached up to tweak my nipple in response.

"Oh man." He tried to catch his breath. "How's that supposed to keep me from blowing my load."

"Because I'll stop you before that happens."

I pushed myself all the way down on his cock so he was buried as deep as he could get—at least for the moment.

The cries he made sounded like he was coming, but he wasn't. Not yet. I moved up and down on his shaft.

"Jordan, you're making me crazy."

"Good." I was almost as out of breath as he was.

As great as my ass felt, my cock was getting a good tease each time I sat and it brushed against his furry abs. It was the perfect caress combined with intense flashes of pleasure pulsing through me from being filled by Miles.

As I got used to him, I was able to pick up the speed. He was a quivering mass beneath me, unable to speak and at times not even able to keep his eyes open. I wasn't much better as I was experiencing the most amazing fuck I'd ever had. I knew I'd be able to give him the ride of his life, but I was giving myself a helluva good time too.

"How you doing down there?" I asked when I needed to be still for a moment.

"Amazing." He focused his eyes on me.

I started riding him fast and deep. I varied the speed, depth, and tightness as much as I could. I was close to losing control and soon nothing was going to stop us from releasing. Miles started thrusting, pushing us closer to the edge.

"Can we?" he asked after a few moments.

He was gorgeous with a sheen of sweat covering him. I couldn't form words anymore, so I nodded. I drove myself down hard on his cock. We both cried out. I stroked my cock fiercely as Miles clenched the sheets with his hands. He pounded me deep, and it wasn't long before I unleashed across his chest. Moments later, he unloaded in the latex sheath that surrounded his pulsing dick.

As soon as we stopped shaking, I gently lifted off Miles's cock and dropped myself on the bed next to him.

"My God, you weren't kidding about your skills," he said as I snuggled next to him.

"Glad you enjoyed it." I kissed his shoulder since it was what was nearest to me and I really couldn't move. "We'll do it again sometime."

"I hope so. You can't do that to me just once." He was quiet for a moment. "Maybe you could teach me how to do it to you?"

"Yes. Absolutely."

My stomach rumbled, making us both laugh.

"I'm right there with you," Miles said. "My stomach will speak up anytime now. That took a lot out of me. How about we clean up and make some food?"

"And talk."

"Yes, and talk."

TWENTY-ONE

We decided on omelets, potatoes, and toast. It might be evening, but breakfast was exactly the meal we wanted after our bedroom workout.

Miles worked on the omelet ingredients—scallions, cheddar, button mushrooms—and I tackled getting potatoes shredded. Working side by side was comfortable and enjoyable. So far, either we'd gone out or he'd surprised me by cooking. This was domesticity as if we'd been together for months instead of a couple of weeks.

"You're really into the cooking," I said as I prepped the potatoes. "I love it. I don't cook at home as much as I should."

"I usually only eat out for special occasions. I find this relaxing at the end of the day. Plus I like to stay on my game because there's a few of us that get together for a recipe-trading potluck. Luke and his wife, along with three others and me get together twice a month. It's not like some of the bigger winter potlucks, but we have a fun time finding new dishes for one another. If you're up here when we're doing one, you'll have to come."

"I'd like that." I picked up the pace on the potatoes since our stomachs were calling out more often. "So how do you want to do this?"

"Well, I was figuring just frying with some salt and pepper. Did you—"

I laughed as I lit the burner and set the pan down with some butter in it. "I got the potatoes. I meant us. Here versus Chicago. Figuring out what we are—friends with some killer benefits or are we becoming a couple?"

Miles got sausage from the fridge and crumbled it into a pan while I let the silence hang. It was easy since I had the distraction of staring at his hot ass in the sweatpants he wore.

"From the first time we talked about the future, we knew we wanted to stay friends." He minded his skillet as he talked. "I almost wrecked everything because of my pride...."

"Hold on, let's be clear, you didn't almost wreck anything. It was me keeping a secret that made it go sideways. I knew your prideful tendencies and shouldn't have tried to get around them."

I looked from him to the potatoes, wanting to make sure I got the right sear on the bottom layer.

"Fair enough. I want to make sure we stay friends. But, I'd like more." I nodded because we seemed to be on the same page. "People make long distance work all the time."

"But how does that work at the beginning like this?"

He shrugged. "We go back and forth. A lot."

"I'm game for that. Not only have I fallen for you, but I'm loving the island too. I'm not sure what it'll be like when it's cold enough for that ice bridge you've talked about. But, I'm into how things move here—the slower pace, the beauty of it all. I suspect you've only shown me a small part."

I managed to flip the entire skillet of potatoes over with minimal spillage on the stove.

"Look at you. I've never had the guts to try that."

"I can do it with potatoes, pancakes, and veggies. I'll teach you sometime." I steered us back on topic. "Anyway, I'd love to come up here more. With an internet connection, I can work from anywhere, and Chicago's close enough that I can get back for meetings when I need to. Hell, maybe I'll learn to fly and just buy a plane for us to use."

I suddenly lost him. He looked past me and out the window that was over the kitchen sink. I was kinda joking about the plane, although it might make sense if there was a lot of travel. It was something to look into one day.

"What?" I started moving the potatoes around since the other side should be browned. He added mushrooms to the sausage.

"You realize there's a huge discrepancy in how we live, right? And not just city versus island. I have the feeling you make significantly more than I do. I live just fine." He waved his hand, indicating the house. "But I live within my means despite what it may look like with the business. What happens when you want to do something I can't afford? You can't pay my way all the time."

The potatoes were done, so I dropped the burner to low so they'd stay warm.

"I'm in love with you." I stood behind him, arms around his shoulders in a hug. "I don't care what your net worth is. I told you, I'm not rich. I'm planning for a good retirement, like your parents did. I save for a rainy day and to support a family when the time comes. Sometimes I do frivolous things, but it's not my every day."

He put his spoon aside and placed his hands on mine. I

gave him a moment to see if he was going to talk, but he didn't.

"I'm not going to shower you with gifts," I continued. "Am I going to spend some money to come up here? Yes. Will I help you with money? Yes. But only if you ask. I won't keep secrets about money again."

He nodded and seemed more at ease.

"I should get started on the omelets before we pass out from hunger." He busied himself for a moment before getting back to the discussion. "You know, though, I won't be taking you on flashy dates."

"You're kidding, right? I was serious when I told you that you'd set the bar high. Sunrise, sunset, the beautiful first night I was here. That was all incredible. I'm really a pretty simple guy."

"A simple guy who can save businesses without breaking a sweat."

"And you teach people how to ride horses and transport people all over this island. We've each got our thing."

"True. We're gonna give this a go, aren't we?" He sprinkled ingredients into the eggs that were already setting up in the pan.

"I think we should." I nestled against his back, careful not to impede his cooking. "I want to feel like this all the time. I feel connected to you in a way I haven't to anyone else." I dropped to almost a whisper. "I think you might be my Richard. The world just seems right since I met you."

He turned his head and we kissed.

"Does that mean you have to be Elise?" He winked at me before he turned back to the stove.

"Okay, so maybe we're each other's Richard."

"I'm good with that." He flipped both omelets with a

spatula. "Can you grab some plates? We're just about ready to serve."

I got going with my tasks. "What do you want to do with the rest of the evening?"

"I was thinking remake the bed and curl up in it again. Maybe go for a second round?"

"I'm for anything that lets us get naked and next to each other."

"How long can you stay?"

"No idea. I've got a couple days of clothes at the inn, but I can buy stuff to stay longer. I'll talk to Alberto in the morning to figure out what the reality is. The most important thing today was just to get here."

"We'll figure it out," he said as he plated the food.

"Yes, we will."

EPILOGUE

One Year Later

I waited as the ferry came in and passengers disembarked. It wasn't as gorgeous as last year because clouds rolled in, but I couldn't complain. It'd been raining in Chicago when I'd left earlier in the week so this was an improvement.

The ferry was full, which wasn't a surprise since it was once again *Somewhere in Time* weekend and the festivities would begin tomorrow. As I waited by the carriage, familiar people came my way.

"Melanie, George." I waved as they approached. "I wondered if you'd all be here. It's good to see you."

"Jordan," Melanie said, coming up and giving me a hug. "How wonderful."

"Hope you'll join me in a round or two again," George said as we shook hands.

"At least one, for sure. Angie, Cathy, welcome back. And who is this?" I looked at the young man holding Cathy's hand.

"This is Taylor," Cathy said proudly. "My boyfriend and recent convert to the awesomeness of the movie."

"Good to meet you, Taylor."

He gave a nod of his head. I wasn't sure he was as much of a convert as Cathy wanted him to be, but she was happy.

"His parents are coming up later today, but the lovebirds decided to come ahead with us."

"Mom," Cathy said with the teenage tone that cautioned against embarrassing them.

"How did we miss you on the ferry?" Melanie asked, ignoring her daughter.

"I was here already." I scanned the crowd to make sure everyone was off the ferry. "Looks like you get the carriage to yourselves since the other one's already headed to the hotel."

The look of confusion Melanie and George traded made me smile.

"I'm helping Miles out this weekend. I live up here part-time now."

"Does that mean...?" Melanie trailed the question off.

I nodded and grinned big, as I did anytime I talked about Miles. "It's an anniversary for us since it was this time a year ago that we met."

She hugged me again, more aggressively this time. "Oh my goodness. A real-life romance. You'll have to let us toast you two to help celebrate."

"That would be wonderful. Let's get you on your way so you can check in."

"You drive this thing now?" Angie asked.

"That I do," I said as I helped the ladies into the carriage.

Once they were settled, I hopped up front and got us moving. I'd become a pretty good rider over the past year.

Buttercup was now designated as my horse for solo rides. I'd also learned how to drive the carriages so I could help out when needed. Since I was an investor, in more ways than one now, it only made sense to lend a hand. I had no idea I'd enjoy working outside as much as I did during the summer. I'd given as much time as I could to the stables without neglecting my regular job.

"So you're up here in the winter too?" Cathy asked.

"I'm usually here every other week. More if I can. There were some intense weeks in the cold. But the ice bridge formed right after Valentine's Day, and that was very cool."

Taylor asked what that was, and I gave him the usual rundown that the tourists were all curious about.

"I wanna see that," he said. "Sounds amazing."

"Come on up. We'd be happy to host."

"I think winter's already too cold," Melanie said. "I don't think I need to see an ice bridge."

"I've got some pictures and video on my phone. I'll let you see them from the warmth of the dining room."

"That'll do me just fine," she said. "So you and Miles—"

"It took us a few weeks to sort things out after the convention last year, but we did and it's been great ever since. Living in two places isn't always easy, but I think we're doing good. I've got an office in his house so I can work when I'm here, plus I work with him. He's in Chicago for a few days every couple of months when he can leave his staff to handle things. We talk, some would say way too much, when we're in different cities."

"Wonderful. I can't wait to congratulate him."

"He's been out with an early tour group and should just be getting back. He's also doing a presentation on Saturday to show some of his father's photos."

"I saw his father do that presentation the first time we came up here," she said. "It'll be great to see those again."

"There're some great images for sure. And here we are." We started up the Grand's driveway. "Welcome to the Grand Hotel."

I brought us to a stop just behind the other carriage that had come from the ferry. On the porch stood Miles and Alberto, who must've arrived while I was at the docks. I waved to them before I hopped down to assist my passengers.

"Look who I found," I called up to Miles as I held Melanie's hand while she stepped down.

Miles clapped Alberto on the shoulder and motioned for him to follow. "Melanie, George. Terrific," he said as he came down the stairs.

We traded a quick kiss hello before he greeted everyone else.

"And this is my business partner, Alberto Belasco. I met this awesome family last year." I took Miles's hand in mine as I made introductions. We matched Taylor and Cathy, who hadn't seemed to let go of each other since they got off the boat.

"Like I told Jordan, we're so happy for you two," Melanie said. "I want to hear all the stories."

"We're going to be late, Mom, if we don't get going." Angie sounded worried.

"Yes, we've decided on spa treatments to get us fully relaxed. I'm not sure what these two are up to"—she motioned to George and Taylor—"but we're checking in and then off to be pampered."

"We'll see you later then," Miles said as the family headed for the lobby.

I turned to Alberto and gave him a quick hug. "I didn't know you were coming in so early."

"Yeah, I said fuck it and just decided to get here. I was hanging out on the porch when Miles came up and now here you are."

"I've got to prep for another tour that leaves in an hour," Miles said. "You should come, if you're not doing anything."

"Me?" Alberto asked. "On a horse? I haven't ridden any other time I've been up here. Why would I do it now?"

"Because it's awesome," I said. "Why do you think we keep asking you to do it? Tell you what, I'll come along too."

"And I promise you won't be the only newbie there. There's at least three other first-timers."

"If it makes you feel better, I'll let you ride Buttercup. She's never done wrong by me."

"Fine," Alberto relented. "But if I get hurt, it's on you two."

"Understood," I said.

I took Miles's hand as we walked back to the Grand's stables. It was perfect how the anniversary of our meeting was tied to this most romantic of all weekends. I loved what we'd made of our life so far. *Somewhere in Time* showed a love that spanned decades. We were only past the first year, but I looked forward to making our decades—with no rogue pennies, or anything else, pulling us out of it.

AUTHOR'S NOTE

I have vivid childhood memories of going up to Mackinac with my mom and grandfather, riding in his four-seater Cessna plane and landing on the Island to spend the day. I was enamored of the horses on the streets, the buildings (which were nothing like we had in Flint) and the amazing fudge. In later life, one of the reasons I fell in love with the film *Somewhere in Time* was because the majority of it was set on Mackinac. I had a great time using both the island and the film to create this story of two men finding love.

To the readers who've seen *Somewhere in Time*, I hope you enjoy this book, which, in some ways, is a love letter to the film. Be advised that if you haven't seen it there are spoilers ahead. However, don't let that detract you from giving the movie a try. I admit that it's not for everyone but it's worth giving it a shot for Christopher Reeve and Jane Seymour if nothing else.

Thanks to the crew who helped me with this story. My husband, Will, is always a great collaborator and reader. He provided ideas on how to make this better and I thank him for that. My writing group—Aaron, Brian, Chris, and Elvis—offered valuable feedback on a couple of early chapters. Thanks also to Kiki Clark at Les Court Author Services who helped me brush this up for its second edition.

ALSO BY JEFF ADAMS

Hockey Romance

Head in the Game

The Hockey Player's Heart (co-written with Will Knauss)

The Hockey Player's Snow Day

Keeping Kyle (A Hockey Allies Bachelor Bid Romance)

Rivals

On Stage Romance Series

Dancing for Him

Love's Opening Night

More Romances

A Sound Beginning

Bicycle Built for Two

Room Service

Somewhere on Mackinac

Summer Heat

Young Adult Titles

Each of these are available in ebook, paperback and audiobook

Codename: Winger series

Tracker Hacker (includes the bonus short story *A Very Winger Christmas*)

Schooled

Audio Assault

Netminder

Other Young Adult Titles

Flipping for Him

ABOUT THE AUTHOR

Jeff Adams has written stories since he was in middle school and became a published author in 2009 when his first short stories were published. He writes both gay romance and LGBTQ young adult fiction...and there's usually a hockey player at the center of the story.

Jeff lives in central California with his husband of more than twenty years, Will. Some of his favorite things include the musicals *Rent* and *[title of show]*, the Detroit Red Wings and Pittsburgh Penguins hockey teams, and the reality TV competition *So You Think You Can Dance*. He, of course, loves to read, but there isn't enough space to list out his favorite books.

Jeff and Will are also podcasters. The *Big Gay Fiction Podcast* is a weekly show devoted to gay romance as well as pop culture. New episodes come out weekly at BigGayFictionPodcast.com.

Learn more about Jeff, his books and find his social media links at JeffAdamsWrites.com. From the website you can also sign up for his newsletter to get a free ebook of *The Hockey Player's Snow Day*, as well serialized stories, previews of new books, book recommendations and more!

Milton Keynes UK
Ingram Content Group UK Ltd.
UKHW011815020224
437175UK00011B/1155